S0-AKL-513

Annie turned, expecting a frown but finding a wry smile instead. "Yeah, probably not what you really want to be doing."

"I didn't say that."

"But you were thinking it."

"So now you're a mind reader?" Ian raised his eyebrows.

"No." She dropped her gaze. He always used to say that when she would tell him what he was supposedly thinking. Why did she have to keep remembering things from their past?

Ian headed for the door, then turned. "Let's drop these documents off with Melody."

Unlike Melody, he didn't outpace Annie. Did he remember her short legs couldn't keep up with his long strides? He used to call her "short stuff" and would stand with his chin resting on the top of her head to prove it. Another recollection. How was she going to overcome the constant barrage of memories?

"You know," he said as they walked, "just because I think it's better for someone else to represent you in court doesn't mean I'm going to turn my back on you completely."

He didn't say it, but he might as well have finished the sentence with "like you did to me."

Books by Merrillee Whren

Love Inspired

The Heart's Homecoming
An Unexpected Blessing
Love Walked In
The Heart's Forgiveness
Four Little Blessings
Mommy's Hometown Hero
Homecoming Blessings
*Hometown Promise
*Hometown Proposal
*Hometown Dad
Montana Match
†Second Chance Reunion

*Kellerville
†Village of Hope

MERRILLEE WHREN

is the winner of a 2003 Golden Heart Award, presented by Romance Writers of America, for best inspirational romance manuscript. In 2004 she made her first sale to Love Inspired Books. She is married to her own personal hero, her husband of thirty-plus years, and has two grown daughters. She has lived in Atlanta, Boston, Dallas and Chicago but now makes her home on one of God's most beautiful creations, an island off the east coast of Florida. When she's not writing or working for her husband's recruiting firm, she spends her free time playing tennis or walking the beach, where she does the plotting for her novels. Please visit her website, merrilleewhren.com.

Second Chance Reunion

Merrillee Whren

HARLEQUIN® LOVE INSPIRED®

Recycling programs
for this product may
not exist in your area.

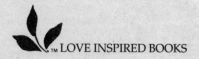

™ LOVE INSPIRED BOOKS

ISBN-13: 978-0-373-81812-9

Second Chance Reunion

Copyright © 2015 by Merrillee Whren

www.Harlequin.com

Printed in U.S.A.

Above all, love each other deeply,
because love covers over a multitude of sins.
—*1 Peter* 4:8

This book is dedicated to Bev and Dan Fritz, who spent many years working at Cookson Hills Christian Ministries. I would also like to thank Jeanette Soltys Quinlan for her help with family law in Georgia. All mistakes are mine.

Chapter One

Doubts crowded Annie Payton's mind as she paced in front of the windows looking out on The Village of Hope's campus. Redbrick buildings with white Georgian columns formed a quadrangle around an expansive lawn. Tall pines and majestic oaks accented with maples and flowering dogwoods added to the beauty of the scenery.

She always loved early spring in Georgia, when the dogwoods dressed the landscape in lace. The pleasant warmth of a late-March afternoon helped to take away some of her anxiety as she waited to meet with the lawyer who hopefully could help her get her kids back. Could this place really return hope to her life?

The scent of newly mowed grass wafted through the open window. Closing her eyes, she breathed deeply and wished she could mow down all the bad things in her life and make it fresh and new. But isn't that what God had done when He'd covered her sins with His grace? Why did she doubt that God had forgiven her?

The click of the door on the far side of the room made Annie turn and look. A man, with his back to her, talked with someone in the hallway. Annie braced herself for this meeting and prayed that the decision to come here was a wise one.

When the man faced her, Annie gasped. What was Ian Montgomery doing here?

"Hello, Annie." He looked as handsome as ever with his sandy-blond hair and gray eyes that reminded her of a stormy sky. Those eyes held no welcome.

Her pulse thundered all over her body. She swallowed hard. "You're the lawyer?"

"The one and only." He motioned toward the chair in front of his desk. "Have a seat."

Like an automaton, Annie sat on the black leather chair. Why did Ian have to be the one person who could help her get what she wanted most in life? Pastor John from the rehab facility often told her things happened for a reason. Could God use this meeting with Ian for good, too?

Annie sat there, not knowing what to say.

Ian broke the silence. "You're looking good."

Annie wanted to tell him he looked great in his dark pin-striped suit, but she thought better of it. "Thanks. I'm feeling good, too. I've been clean and sober for a year and twenty days. I intend to stay that way."

"I'm glad for your sobriety, but I have to be honest, Annie. You told me that several times before, and you didn't follow through."

"I know." Annie smiled halfheartedly. Everything he said was true, and he had the right to doubt her statement. She would show him that his doubts were unfounded this time.

Ian gave her a look that told her she would have to work hard to prove she had changed. "I understand Melody Hammond, our women's ministry director, has explained our program and gotten you settled in an apartment."

"She has. She said I have more paperwork to fill out."

His gray eyes narrowed. "I hope Melody also told you I only have a few minutes with you today."

"She did. She said you have an important meeting to attend."

Nodding, Ian grimaced. "The quarterly board meeting."

"You don't look too excited."

"Let's just say it's not one of my favorite things." Ian tapped the file on his desk. "You want your kids back. That's what we need to discuss."

Annie nodded, a lump forming in her throat at the thought of Kara and Spencer. Her babies were nearly four and three—babies no longer, but she'd missed a whole year of their lives. She longed to hold them in her arms, kiss them and tuck them into bed at night. Could she ever make it up to them? She promised herself she would get her kids back. She would.

"How long have Kara and Spencer been in foster care?"

"Over a year. DFCS took them away…" Annie stopped as her voice cracked. She pressed her lips together as she tried to regain her composure. She wouldn't cry in front of Ian. "I was more messed up than ever, but losing the kids made me realize I had to get help and get it right this time. I want to reunite my family."

"Annie, I don't know whether I can help you. I have to be sure you're going to stay sober before I can. Besides, I don't feel comfortable being your attorney considering our past relationship."

"But Melody said the lawyer here would help me. Since you're the only one, doesn't that mean you have to represent me?"

"Not necessarily. I have a friend who can probably take your case."

"I can't afford to pay someone."

"He volunteers his services here from time to time."

Annie breathed a sigh of relief, but her heart ached because Ian didn't believe she could stay clean. Could she blame him? He'd seen her relapse too many times, but this time was different. "When will I get to talk with him?"

"I'll arrange a meeting as soon as I can." Ian stood as he picked up the file folder and headed for the door. "I'm sorry I have to go. We can talk again later after I contact Scott Bartlett, the other attorney. I'll set up a time for the three of us to meet."

"So this is it? Hi and goodbye?" Annie followed Ian to the door. He had a meeting, but his eagerness to be rid of her punched a hole in her heart.

"That's the way it has to be today. Melody wanted me to talk to you, so I agreed." He put his hand on the doorknob.

"She doesn't know about us, does she? Does anyone here know?" Annie couldn't believe she was confronting Ian this way. Was she trying to alienate him?

Staring at her, Ian took his hand from the doorknob. "That's a fair question. Adam Bailey, the administrator here, knows everything, but no one else. I'm not going out of my way to talk about my former wild life."

"Guess my presence is going to open up your past whether you like it or not." Annie wondered why she continued to needle him. Maybe it was a defensive mechanism. She needed to keep him at an emotional distance because his presence aroused old feelings that were better buried and forgotten.

"You're probably right, but I'll deal with it in my

own way. You don't have to worry about it." Ian opened the door and held out a hand. "After you."

"Thanks." Annie stepped into the hallway.

Ian closed the door behind him. "I'll be in contact."

"Okay." Annie stood there, not knowing what to do now.

Ian looked as if he were going to dismiss her as he walked into the hallway, but then he turned back. "Walk with me," he said.

His request caught her off guard, but she was grateful he didn't dismiss her as they headed toward the reception area. "Sure."

"Do your parents know you're out of rehab?"

So that's what he wanted. More information. He didn't really want to walk with her. "No. My parents haven't spoken to me in over three years. For all they know I could be dead."

"Are you sure about that?"

She nodded, not wanting to think about the parents who had abandoned her. They'd called it *tough love,* but Annie called it *no love.* Could she ever prove to them that she had changed? She had to show them all that she had. Ian. Her parents. The court.

"Annie, if you need help, talk to Melody. As the director of the women's ministry, she's here to give you advice while you settle in. This is a good place for you to find your way again."

Annie forced a smile. "Thanks. I guess I'll see you later. Hope your meeting goes well."

"Thanks. Me, too." He smiled in return.

Annie nodded and hurried away with the image of Ian's smile filling her thoughts. She didn't want that smile to make her think he might care about her on a personal level. That kind of thinking could only lead her to more heartache. She'd had more than her share, and she had no one to blame but herself.

Annie forced herself not to run or to look back at Ian. The whole meeting with him had been surreal. He'd been so matter-of-fact. He obviously didn't have any remnants of those long-ago feelings they'd shared. To a casual observer, his demeanor would have given no hint that he'd been talking to his ex-wife.

Standing at the edge of the reception area, Ian observed Annie as she slipped out of the administration building without a backward glance. Against his will, he watched her through the glass door as she meandered down the walkway. When she was gone from his sight, he let out a harsh breath. He could hardly believe he'd remained so calm during their meeting. The last time they'd seen each other a rancorous conversation had ensued. He couldn't let even a hint of old feelings enter his mind. Annie and he were history.

Ian wasn't sure what he was going to do. How was he supposed to deal with his ex-wife? He had to treat her like any other resident. But was that possible? Emotions of every stripe flooded his mind. How could he ever focus on the board meeting after this conversation with her?

How could he consider helping her reunite with her children when he didn't trust her? He'd been burned before by her pledges. Her two sweet children didn't deserve to be manipulated by the promises their mother never kept. But she'd been in rehab for a year, and John Rice didn't put up with misbehavior at his rehab center, so maybe she was clean. But could she stay that way?

Ian looked heavenward. "Why now, Lord? Why when I need to have my focus on keeping this place going? What do you want me to do with Annie?"

"Are you talking to yourself again, Mr. Ian?" The sound of Lovie Trimble's voice floated his way.

Ian jerked his head toward the sound. "Saying a prayer ahead of the board meeting. I didn't see you there."

"I was delivering a message and returned just in time to hear you muttering." She shook her head as she settled in her chair behind the reception desk. "That board meeting must have you in a dither."

Ian smiled, knowing Lovie had no idea what had him talking to himself and offering prayers for help. "It's a big meeting. Have any of the board members arrived yet?"

A wide grin wrinkling her face, she glanced at the clock on the wall opposite the desk. "Not yet, but I expect they'll arrive any minute. Hope all goes well. Adam seemed a little on edge about it."

"He has a lot riding on this. Lots of important decisions may happen today." Ian nodded. "Put on your prayer warrior bonnet and start praying."

Her chocolate-brown eyes twinkled. With her silver-gray hair, she looked like the queen bee behind the reception desk. "I've been praying for you two daily since the meeting was scheduled."

"I should've known. You're one of the people who puts 'hope' in The Village of Hope."

"I think that description fits you and Adam, too."

"I'd like to think so, but no one can beat you. You're the face of hope when people walk in this front door." Ian made a wide gesture around the entrance hall with its shiny marble floor and the two-story ceiling.

"Now you're making me blush." Lovie waved a hand at Ian. "Go on to your meeting before I wish I were thirty years younger and could end your bachelor days. Be warned. I'm on the lookout for a good match for you."

"Forget the matchmaking. I've had my chance at love, and it didn't work out."

Lovie shook her head. "There are always second

chances. When the right gal comes along and catches one glimpse of your Ryan Gosling good looks, she'll win your heart."

"I don't need a woman. And quit comparing me to some movie star."

"How can I help it when you look just like him?"

Ian rolled his eyes. "That's debatable."

"I saw you staring after that cute young woman with that dark hair and blue, blue eyes who just left. She might be a good match for you."

Ian shook his head. "Lovie, what am I going to do with you? You can't keep trying to match me up with every woman who walks in the door."

"Sure I can." Lovie chuckled.

Ian sighed. "Guess I can't stop you. Got to get to that meeting. See you later."

Turning on his heel, Ian headed for the conference room while Lovie's laughter followed him down the hall. Wouldn't she have a ball if she knew Annie was his ex-wife? He shook the thought away. He needed his focus on the upcoming meeting, not Annie.

With that thought in mind, Ian hurried toward the room where the board would meet. A silent prayer for a positive outcome formed in his mind as he entered.

Glad to be the first one here, he navigated past a large oak table surrounded by a dozen chairs in the center of the room. He stopped in front of the row of windows overlooking the campus quad. Like the spokes of a wheel, sidewalks radiated out from a fountain toward the buildings around the quad. He loved this place. He prayed again that nothing would happen to close it down. Too many people depended on the services provided here. Even Annie.

Footsteps sounded behind Ian. He turned and greeted two members of the board as they found seats at the table. Before they could converse further, several other men entered the room. The area filled with greetings, laughter and backslapping as the others found places to sit. Ian nodded to acknowledge the others who had joined them. After Melody and Adam entered the room, everyone settled in, and Ian pulled his notes from a folder.

Melody squeezed her chair in next to Ian's and leaned closer. "How did your meeting with Annie go?"

Ian shrugged. "Okay. Did you talk to her again?"

"There wasn't time."

"True." Ian wondered how he could've asked such a stupid question. He'd better get his thoughts in order. "We can confer later."

After Adam opened the meeting with prayer, Ian surveyed the four women and eight men who comprised the board of directors. These folks had had a vision several years ago to turn this abandoned college campus on the outskirts of Atlanta into a place to minister to folks who needed a helping hand. Over the past year, they seemed to have lost the vision.

The meeting started with the mundane reports that always characterized such gatherings. After the reports and old business concluded, Bob Franklin, the board chairman, introduced new business. Ian held his breath. This was the subject he didn't want to hear.

Bob cleared his throat. "I know some of you won't like what I have to say, but it has to be said. This institution is in the red. Donations are down, way down. How can we be good stewards if we continue to pile on debt? I propose we end this ministry and try to sell the property—have an auction if we can't find a buyer in the traditional way."

Adam stood at the opposite end of the table. "What will happen to the people who live here and depend on what we have to offer?"

Bob raised his eyebrows. "We can refer them to other charitable organizations."

Ian stood beside Adam. "Do you intend to make a formal motion to that effect?"

Bob glanced around the table. "Not now. I'd like to hear what everyone has to say."

Ian forced himself not to jump in with his opinion. He resumed his seat. *Patience. Persistence. Prayer.* He let the words roll through his thoughts as he listened to each of the board members give their views. After all the board members had spoken, Ian had a big knot in his stomach. Only five of the members implied they wanted to keep The Village open. So if it came down to a vote today, things didn't look good.

After looking over the group, Bob's gaze settled on Ian. "Would y'all like to say something?"

"I'll let Melody speak." Ian gestured toward her.

Melody stood, her posture exuding confidence. "Thanks. When I took the women's ministries co-ordinator job, I didn't know how much this place would come to mean to me. But this isn't about me. It's about the hundreds of women who've been saved from abuse, who've found jobs and a better life. You can't let a financial setback end this ministry. Remember what Jesus said in Luke. 'What is impossible with man is possible with God.'"

When Melody returned to her seat, Adam stood. "Melody has given you only one of the reasons why we should continue. Have we lost the vision that started this ministry?"

Ian stood. Leaning forward, he placed his palms on the table and stared at the group. "Isn't this where faith comes in? Remember the story of the Israelites when they crossed the Jordon River and conquered Jericho. The priests stepped into the river on faith, and they were able to cross the river on dry ground. The people marched around Jericho and the walls fell. Why can't we have faith like that?"

No one said a thing. A mower outside sounded loud in the quiet room. Trying to gauge the response of the individual board members, he let his gaze roam from face to face until it rested on Bob Franklin. Bob stood, his expression giving no clue to his thoughts.

Bob folded his arms across his trim waist. "You make a good point, Ian, but sometimes we have to count the cost, too. Don't you agree?"

Adam held his hands out, palms up. "What about giving us a few months to work on the budget and develop some more financial partners. Can we agree on that?"

Ian had always admired Adam's spiritual sense. "Adam's right. Let's see where we stand at the next board meeting in three months."

A cacophony of voices erupted in the room. Bob banged his gavel. The roar dwindled to a murmur. Finally, quiet reigned.

Bob walked around the table until he was standing next to Ian. "What about your dad getting his church behind the ministry?"

Ian wondered where this line of thinking was headed. "His church already makes a monthly donation."

"I know, but I mean making The Village of Hope a primary concern, not just one of dozens of ministries they support." Bob narrowed his gaze as he looked at Ian. "I'm sure you could persuade your dad to do that."

Didn't this guy know Ian and his father tended to be on the opposite sides of too many issues? Probably not. It wasn't like the differences between father and son were common knowledge. Ian had dishonored his parents with his previous behavior, and his dad had never quite gotten over it.

Ian wasn't sure he even knew how to approach his dad, the lead pastor at one of the area's big mega churches. They did a lot of spiritual good in the community, but Ian had always preferred to worship with a small group here at the little chapel. Sometimes people got lost in big congregations, or they could drift and never grow spiritually. He shouldn't judge, but he and Annie were a product of that drift.

The last thing Ian wanted to do was talk to his father about the financial needs of this ministry. But if it meant keeping the doors to The Village of Hope open, Ian would do whatever it took. Too many people depended on this place. He wouldn't let it go under without a fight.

Ian looked the chairman in the eye. "I'll discuss this with my dad, but that's not the only thing I have in mind. Things will be different at the next board meeting. You can count on it."

During her first day at The Village, loneliness invaded Annie's heart and every corner of her tiny apartment—her new home. *Home.* The word went straight to Annie's heart. She hadn't had a real home in years. Getting this apartment ready for her kids was a priority. She took a deep breath. The smell of pine-scented cleaning fluid filled the air. The rehab facility had been clean, but this place gleamed from floor to ceiling. She hated to think of the squalor she'd once lived in. Never would she live like that again.

Clean. A clean start. A clean life. A clean conscience.

Tempted to turn on the ancient TV for company, Annie couldn't think of a thing she wanted to watch. She surveyed the apartment's Spartan furnishings—a sofa covered in a plain blue slipcover that matched the single chair sitting at an angle in the corner. A small round wooden table and four ladder-back chairs sat in front of the opening to the galley kitchen.

Annie went into the kitchen and ran a hand across the smooth laminate countertops that mixed golds, browns and grays, mimicking the granite in her mother's designer kitchen. Annie longed to have Kara and Spencer with her and add a few personal touches to the place. That couldn't happen until she had some money. And that meant finding a job. Would Melody be able to help in that regard?

Taking a deep breath, Annie tried to dwell on God's promises. She should be grateful she had a place to live and people willing to give her assistance. But Ian's less-than-enthusiastic welcome blunted the other good things about this place. She couldn't blame him. How could he forgive her for choosing a life of decadence over him?

Annie jumped up as a knock sounded on the door. Did she dare hope it was Ian coming to tell her he'd changed his mind about representing her? Wishful thinking.

Annie looked through the viewer in the door. A distorted image of Melody came into Annie's vision. Her heart sank.

Manufacturing a smile, she opened the door. "Come in."

"Thanks. Are you getting settled?" Melody set her portfolio and cell phone on the dark brown coffee table that sported a few nicks and dings.

Annie shrugged as she tried to hold her smile in place. "Not much to settle. I don't have very many things."

"Do you mind if I sit down?"

"Oh, sure. I'm sorry I didn't offer you a seat." Annie wished she didn't feel so awkward around this very put together woman.

When Pastor John had arranged for her to meet Melody, Annie had imagined a mother figure, but Melody wasn't the older woman that she'd created in her mind. Melody was young—maybe only a year or two older than Annie.

The other woman's gray business suit, a sharp contrast to Annie's blue jeans and white knit top, reminded Annie of her mother—all business and not much love. Annie longed for a gentle mother figure—something she hadn't had growing up. Her mother had handed Annie and her brother over to nannies and housekeepers. Marcia Payton had always been too busy for her own children.

Annie chastised herself. How could she have such critical feelings about her mother when she'd neglected her own children so much that they'd been taken away? She had no right to judge anyone, least of all her mother. Annie had felt emotional neglect, but nobody reported that to the Division of Family and Children Services. At thirty years of age, why was she worried about having a mother in her life? She should concentrate on being the kind of mother her own children could depend on.

"No need to be sorry." Melody sat on the sofa. "I'd like to get some more information from you so I can help you find a job. That's part of what we do here."

"That's good to know. What information do you need?" Annie hoped it wasn't something she didn't want to talk about.

Before Melody could answer, her cell phone rang. She glanced at it. "I'm sorry. I need to take this call."

"No problem."

Annie sat at the other end of the sofa while Melody spoke in excited tones. Annie gathered that the call brought good news. She wished she could receive good news, too. But hadn't she? She had a wonderful place to live. She should be grateful for the good things and try to move on from the bad. But with the history between her and Ian lying in wait to disrupt everything, she had a hard time being optimistic.

When Melody finished, she looked over at Annie. "Sorry about that. One of my ladies is ready to leave The Village and go out on her own, and someone has donated secondhand furniture for her to use in her new apartment. She'll be so excited."

"That's wonderful for her."

"Yes, it is." Picking up the portfolio, Melody stood. "But, unfortunately for you, I have to meet the folks with the furniture, and that means cutting our meeting short."

"That's okay."

"No, it's not. We need to get things started for you, so someday you can do the same thing—go out on your own."

"We can always do this later." Annie tried to smile. The prospect of being on her own both excited and frightened her.

"There's no point in putting this off when Ian can help you with this paperwork." Melody headed for the door. "I'll drive you over to the administration building so you can meet with him in his office. Then you and Ian can discuss your case further."

Wondering whether she should tell Melody that Ian didn't plan to be her legal counsel, Annie followed the other woman out to her car. Annie got into the passenger seat and decided she would keep her mouth shut. Ian would eventually have to explain everything. "Shouldn't we call him first? Maybe he's busy."

Melody pulled her car to a stop in the parking lot. "Ian is never too busy to help me out. He's there when I need him."

Jealousy erupted in Annie's mind. Did this mean Ian and Melody were involved? Annie chided herself for letting old feelings creep into her thoughts. She'd relinquished any claim on Ian when she'd left him.

"That's good. It's always nice to have someone you can count on." She hadn't been there for Ian. That was part of the reason she was in her current mess. Making a fresh start would be so much easier if he wasn't in the mix. What would he say when she was foisted on him again without warning?

Chapter Two

Annie could barely keep up with Melody as she went through a side door at the end of the hallway where Ian's office was located. Where did Melody get her energy? She walked faster than anyone Annie knew.

Melody tapped on the door, then went into the office without waiting for an invitation. Reluctantly, Annie followed. Ian looked up from his desk and met Annie's gaze. An expression she couldn't define crossed his face. Was he worried she had explained their former relationship to Melody?

Then Ian looked at Melody and smiled. "What can I do for you ladies?"

He had a smile for Melody but not for her. Jealousy slithered back into Annie's heart. She didn't want to feel this way. Nothing good could come from it.

Melody laid papers on his desk. "Could you go

over these with Annie and then show her around campus? I had planned to, but one of my ladies is getting her own place."

Ian smiled again. "Sure. I know how excited you get when that happens. Go. I'll take care of this."

"Thanks. You're a sweetheart." Melody turned to Annie. "I'll check with you after I get back."

Annie nodded, feeling like a hot potato that everyone kept tossing about. She watched Melody leave. Alone with Ian, Annie didn't know what to say or how to act. What was he thinking? Did she dare look at him?

"So here we are again."

Annie turned, expecting a frown but found a wry smile instead. "Yeah, probably not what you really want to be doing."

"I didn't say that."

"But you were thinking it."

"So now you're a mind reader?" He raised his eyebrows.

"No." She dropped her gaze. He always used to say that when she would tell him what he was supposedly thinking. Why did she have to keep remembering things from the past? Why couldn't she look forward, not back?

"Just because I think it's better for someone else to represent you in court doesn't mean I'm going to turn my back on you completely."

He didn't say it, but he might as well have finished the sentence with *like you did to me*. The past barged into her thoughts again. It was as bad as the drugs and alcohol that had once enslaved her. She couldn't shake it. "What do I have to do?"

"Let's see what we've got here." Ian picked up the papers Melody had left. "The usual forms we have new residents fill out so we know your job skills."

"But you know those."

"But Melody doesn't, and she needs this for her records." Ian handed her the papers and a pen. "Fill this out."

Annie skimmed the pages as Ian busied himself with something on his computer. The papers were essentially a job application and a personality test. Annie filled in the information with a renewed hope. Seeing her job experience in writing made her realize she had some marketable skills. But how many employers were willing to take a chance on a former drug addict? The past again. She couldn't banish it from her mind.

"Here." She let out a loud sigh as she finished and handed the papers back to Ian. "I wasn't sure about the contact information for my former bosses."

"That's usually the case with most of our new residents. This is mainly to see what experience you've had so we can help you search for the right kind of employment."

"Okay." Annie sat there, her stomach whirling

with nervous anticipation. "Do you think I'll find a job?"

"With your degree and experience, I'm sure you'll find something." Ian stood. "Now that you've filled these out, let's tour the rest of the campus. We can start in this building, and then I'll point out where all of our other ministries are located."

"I'd like that." Annie jumped up, eager to do something besides sit in Ian's office. Even though being with Ian was difficult, it was better than being alone.

Ian headed for the door, then turned. "We'll drop this stuff off in Melody's office before we start the tour."

Unlike Melody, Ian didn't outpace Annie as they headed down the hallway. Did he remember she had short legs and couldn't keep up with his long strides? He used to call her "short stuff" and would stand with his chin resting on the top of her head to prove it. Another recollection. How was she going to overcome the constant barrage of memories?

He stopped and pushed the envelope through the slot in Melody's office door. When they reached a set of double doors at the opposite end of the hallway from Ian's office, he opened the door for her.

Annie stepped into the cavernous space and took in the floor-to-ceiling mahogany-colored bookcases along three walls. A curved marble staircase hugged the fourth wall and led to the upper floor with an ornately carved balustrade. To the right were the checkout desk and two conference rooms, and on the left two rows of cubicles contained computers and monitors. "Wow! This is fantastic."

"This is the former college library. I knew you'd like it. I remember how you loved to read."

Annie nodded, knowing that was before drugs and alcohol had numbed her brain. She'd begun to read again in rehab, and she wanted desperately to read to her kids and introduce them to the children's books she loved. A spark of surprise that Ian recalled her love of books ignited some happiness. "Do they have a children's section?"

"Absolutely. Back in the far corner." Ian led the way. "Since we have a dozen houses for children, this part of the library gets a lot of use. We'll take a walk through the area where the children's homes are located. We have a day care there, too, where you'll be able to take Spencer and Kara while you're at work."

Ian's positive comment put hope in Annie's heart even though at times it seemed as though he didn't believe his own statements. "I'd love to bring them here."

"And we're going to make that happen."

Annie wanted to believe that was possible. But with Ian passing her off on one of his friends, did he really mean it? Annie straightened her spine and lifted her chin high. "How are you going to make that happen when you won't represent me?"

The urge to take Annie by those stiff shoulders and shake some sense into her zigzagged through Ian's mind, but he crossed his arms in order not to act on the ignoble thought. Why did she have to keep questioning his best wishes for her welfare? How could he convince her that he wanted everything good for her without personally involving himself in her life? That's the last thing either of them needed. He decided it was best to just ignore her question.

"Are you ready to see the rest of what we're doing here at The Village?" Even as Ian made the statement, he feared the time for helping people could come to an end in three months. He wasn't going to let that happen.

"Sure." Annie's stiff stance relaxed and she didn't argue the change in subject.

Ian relaxed, too, and pointed to the left of the administration building. "Good. We'll start in this direction."

"Okay."

Annie's one-word answers told Ian that she wasn't feeling very comfortable with him even though she had appeared to relax. The whole scenario with Annie went beyond surreal. He was here with his ex-wife, and they weren't saying a thing as they walked across the campus. What would his father say if he knew Annie was here?

When they reached the assisted-living facility, Ian introduced Annie to some of the residents who were enjoying a beautiful spring day on the front lawn. He stood back and listened while she chatted nonstop with Cora, one of the elderly ladies. Annie had been very close to her paternal grandparents. When they died suddenly within six months of each other during Annie's junior year in high school, her life had shattered.

Ian had stepped in and offered her comfort, hoping to get close to the young woman he'd admired from afar for months in the church youth group. Little did he know their relationship would shatter his life, too. But he couldn't blame her. He'd been a willing participant in the behavior that eventually nearly killed him and took Annie in a ruinous direction.

"Thanks for bringing this delightful young lady to see me." Cora's comment brought him back from the past.

Ian smiled at Annie, glad she could make a new start where people looked at her with fresh eyes. "You're welcome, Cora, but now I have to take this delightful young lady away because I still have a lot of things to show her."

Cora patted Annie's arm. "Thank you so much, Annie, for stopping and making an old lady's day."

Annie's smile matched the sun beaming overhead. "You made *my* day."

He always loved her smile, but he turned away before he got too caught up in it. Loving anything about Annie Payton was a dangerous thing for him to do. "On to another part of the campus."

"Okay." Annie almost skipped as they made their way toward the children's homes. "Thanks for giving me the time to talk with Cora. I'm going to visit her again."

"She'll be grateful. That's the beauty of this place. We have folks from all walks of life and all ages who can give each other help in a variety of ways. It's truly like a real village."

"I can see that." Annie looked up at him. "You like working here, don't you?"

"I do. It has blessed my life more than I could ever have imagined."

"What does your dad think about it?"

"His church supports it."

"I didn't ask about his church. I asked about him."

Annie's tendency not to hide what she was thinking had been evident from the minute they'd met again. She knew about the disagreements between father and son, and she wasn't going to let Ian slip by with a half answer.

"He's glad I'm doing productive work."

"Somehow I sense a *but* in your statement."

"Okay, you got me there." Ian marveled that Annie could still read the nuances in his words. "Dad thinks I could've made better use of my law degree."

"So he doesn't like you working here?"

"I didn't say that. He supports my work here, but sometimes he has trouble seeing the point of my helping people who frequently find themselves in trouble again."

"People like me."

Ian didn't know how to respond. He wished he hadn't answered her question, but Annie's assessment was exactly right. Sometimes, people took more than one try to get it right. Annie fit that scenario. She seemed determined to stay clean this time. He hated to admit he was more like his dad on Annie's account. She had to prove herself, because she'd fooled him before.

Annie jumped on his nonresponse. "Don't know what to say?"

"Let's not go down that road. We've had a nice time today. Don't ruin it."

Annie's smile faded as she hurried ahead. Ian wasn't going to try to soothe her feelings. Maybe this outing hadn't been such a good idea. When they got back, Melody was sure to be there waiting for a report, and Ian would finally have to tell her about his past. He had to talk to Annie about it.

Annie finally slowed her pace, and Ian caught up to her. "Over your pout?"

"Yeah." She looked up at him again. "I'm beginning to see why you shouldn't be my attorney."

Ian nodded. "I'm glad you're finally seeing it my way. Why the change of heart?"

"There's too much acrimony between us. Too many bad memories that won't go away."

What about the good ones? The thought slipped into Ian's mind. He pushed it away. Annie had assessed the situation correctly. The bad memories far outweighed the good. The truth put a dagger in Ian's heart. As sadness welled up inside of him, he sighed. "And I have to talk to Melody about it."

"Should I be there, too?"

"I think it's best if I do that alone." Ian didn't want Annie to hear some of the things he would say. She didn't need to hear a lot of negative stuff about herself, but it would probably have to be said in the course of the conversation he would have with Melody.

"I suppose so."

While they walked by a playground where a group of children played with abandon, Ian prayed this work wouldn't be disrupted because of financial problems. Where would these people go? What was worse than having the ministry end? Having Annie see it fall apart just after she'd gotten here. If the facility went under, how would the loss affect her life? Would she stay strong or buckle at the first temptation to return to her former life?

Ian didn't want to find out.

"Is this the area where you have the children's homes?" Annie pointed toward the cluster of homes on two cul-de-sac streets.

"Yes, these used to be college faculty homes, and they converted nicely to twelve homes for children. Each one has six kids. The house parents are fabulous people."

"Yeah, I guess so. Six kids is a lot to handle." A cloud of sadness drifted over Annie's face as she gazed up at him. "I couldn't even deal with two. How will Spencer and Kara ever forgive me?"

Ian wished he knew. "I can't answer that."

"I know, but Kara was only three and Spencer two when they went into foster care, and I've only seen them a few times in the past year." Tears welled in Annie's eyes, but she blinked them back as she pressed her lips together.

"When you're reunited with them, it won't take long for them to bond with you again." He hoped that would comfort her. She was trying not to cry, and the sight of her on the verge of tears pulled at his heartstrings. He didn't want her plight to produce tender feelings in his thoughts. Such feelings might lead him to care too much. He'd gone down that road before. Never again. It was the road to heartache.

"I hope you're right. Thanks for believing in me."

Did he believe in her? Not completely, but she needed encouraging reinforcement in her life. Right about now he needed God to rescue him. Annie was getting to him. At that moment, he spied Melody's car headed their way. God had perfect timing. "Looks like Melody's back."

Melody rolled down her window as she slowed her sedan. "Ian, we need to talk."

"You get your lady settled?" Ian wondered what was on Melody's mind.

"Yeah, hop in and I'll give you the details."

Ian glanced at Annie. "You want a ride back to your place?"

Annie shook her head. "I think I'll stop by and see Cora again."

"Are you sure?" Ian hoped Annie didn't feel dismissed, but he had to talk with Melody alone.

"I'm sure. You and Melody have stuff to talk about." Annie lifted her eyebrows until they disappeared under her dark fringe of bangs.

"Okay. Talk to you later." Ian got into the car and hoped Melody didn't notice anything odd about Annie's comment or her expression. He had to work up to the conversation he was going to have about his relationship with his ex-wife.

As Ian got into the car with Melody, jealousy crept through Annie's mind again. Stupid, stupid, stupid. She turned away. Why was she feeling this way? She'd pushed Ian out of her life six years ago because they'd wanted different things. They still didn't suit each other. Nothing had changed.

Even if she hadn't gone down the path to her own destruction, they wouldn't have been compatible. Too bad they hadn't recognized that before they'd ventured into a marriage that had lasted barely over a year.

Her misguided thoughts about Ian were just another example of her bad judgment. She was a terrible judge of men, first Ian and then Jesse, the irresponsible man who had fathered her children. Kara and Spencer were the only two good things that man had ever produced. Ian was a much better person than Jesse, but still the wrong man for her. If she were smart, she would forget men altogether. She had to concentrate on getting her kids back even if dealing with Ian was part of that.

While dozens of thoughts tumbled through Annie's head, she continued to wander down the pathway that took her back to the assisted-living facility. A short distance away, she spotted three white-haired ladies sitting in the shade of a big oak tree popping with the new leaves of spring. Cora was still there. Annie quickened her pace.

"Hi, Cora." Annie waved.

Cora smiled, her wrinkled face beaming. "What a surprise. You're back so soon."

"Yeah. Ian had a meeting, so I decided to visit with y'all for a while."

Cora pointed to an empty chair in their circle. "Come join us, and let me introduce you to Ruby and Liz."

Annie sat on the nearby chair. "Nice to meet you ladies."

"Did you have a lovely walk with Mr. Ian?"

Annie forced a smile rather than the frown that nearly puckered her eyebrows. Why did they have to ask about Ian? "He showed me most of the campus until Melody whisked him away."

"I keep waiting for Ms. Melody and Mr. Ian to become an item, but there aren't any sparks there. What do you think?" Cora peered at her friends.

Liz nodded. "I think you're right. No sparks."

"Yep. Not a one." Ruby bobbed her head in unison with Liz.

Annie wasn't sure whether to be happy that these ladies saw nothing happening between Ian and his coworker or jealous that the ladies wished something was happening. She shouldn't be happy or jealous, but she couldn't ignore the sparks that flitted through her mind when Ian was around. They were hard to ignore even if they were one-sided.

"Maybe that poor girl still needs time to get over the death of her fiancé." Ruby's statement brought Annie back to the ladies' conversation.

"Such a tragedy." Cora shook her head as she

looked at Annie. "He was in Afghanistan delivering aid with a Christian group and was killed days before they were scheduled to come home."

Annie didn't know what to say. How did one respond to such a senseless death? Everything she thought of saying sounded inadequate, but she had to say something. "I can't begin to imagine her sorrow."

"None of us can, and I think that's why she throws herself into her work here." Cora rocked in her chair. "She's trying to forget."

Annie had a lot to forget about her past, but her own self-inflicted troubles faded in comparison. She would never look at Melody in the same way again. "That's hard to do."

"You're so right." Ruby reached over and patted Annie's arm. "Tell us about yourself, dear."

After these ladies had extoled Melody's virtues, how could Annie talk about the bad stuff she had done? There was nothing virtuous about her life. "You don't want to hear about me."

"Sure we do. We want to pray for you. So we need to know what to pray about." A knowing smile curved Cora's thin lips, making every wrinkle in her kind face smile. "We know you came to The Village to get help. We're all here for some kind of help, and we can help each other with prayer."

Cora's warm brown eyes beckoned Annie to make a prayer request. "I'm here because I'm trying to get my kids back. Please pray that the court will see that I'm clean and sober for good and deserve to have my children again."

Liz clapped her hands. "Then that's what we'll be praying about—for your little ones' return to you."

"Thank you." Annie blinked back tears, so thankful that Pastor John had sent her here.

All these people at The Village of Hope doing good for others made Annie want to be a better person. She could be a better person, but could she ever be good enough to make up for her past?

Melody pulled her car away from the curb. "How was your time with Annie?"

"Okay. She filled out your papers, and I put them through the mail slot."

"I know. I read them, and that's what I want to talk to you about."

Ian narrowed his gaze and wondered where this was going. "What about them?"

"Don't you see how she can help us?"

"Help us?"

"Did you read her information? Her job experience?"

Ian nodded. "I know her job experience."

Melody cast him a sideways glance as she parked her car. "Then you should realize what a godsend she is."

Ian shook his head and tried to wrap his mind around what Melody was saying. "How so?"

"She was a financial consultant."

"I still don't know what that has to do with us."

"In order to satisfy the naysayers on the board, we need to put a new financial plan in place. We're going to have to get this place in the black. What better person to help us than someone like Annie."

Ian gritted his teeth in order not to say what he was thinking about his ex-wife. There was no way they could let her near the finances of this ministry. She couldn't be trusted. The time had come to tell Melody everything about Annie and him. "We have to talk about this. Your office or mine?"

Melody opened her car door. "Yours is closer."

As they walked to the administration building in silence, Ian tried to figure out how he would start the conversation. Why had he ever thought he'd never have to talk about his former life?

After Ian unlocked the door and let it swing open, he stood aside for Melody to enter. "Have a seat."

Melody sat on one of two black leather guest chairs in front of Ian's desk. "I'm glad you're at least going to consider using Annie's expertise."

Ian sat on the other chair. "I haven't changed my mind. I have reservations about having her involved with the money."

"What aren't you telling me?"

Melody had just handed him an opening. He should jump right in, but he took a few moments to pray. He couldn't do this without God's help.

"Why so hesitant?" Melody's brow furrowed. "You know something about her that I don't. Tell me what it is."

"It's not only about Annie. It's about me, too." Ian took a deep breath. "I'm not going to represent Annie in her efforts to get her kids back."

"Why?"

"It's not a good idea because we have a rather rancorous story. Annie and I were once married."

Mouth dropping open, Melody leaned forward. After several seconds of silence, she eased back in her chair. "Wow! So this is what you wanted to talk about?"

Ian shrugged. "Not exactly, but it has to be done."

"How long were you married?"

"A little over a year, but our relationship goes back to high school."

"You were high school sweethearts?"

"I guess you could say that." Ian wondered how much he should reveal. He didn't have to go into the details about how they'd experimented with sex and drugs at her house while her parents were away. "Anyway, I'm going to ask Scott Bartlett to represent her. It'll work out better that way."

"I suppose you're right." Melody sighed. "Annie

never said a thing to me about your relationship. What does she think about your being here?"

Ian shook his head. "I don't think it matters to her. She walked out on the marriage because she wanted the party life more than she wanted me."

"Is that why you don't trust her?"

Ian stared at Melody's expectant expression. How much did he tell her? How much had Annie told her? "What do you know about Annie's history?"

"I know she was in rehab for a year and that her kids are in foster care. She hasn't said much more than that. Is there more I should know besides the fact that you were married to her?"

Releasing a harsh breath, Ian stared at his desk and prayed for wisdom before looking up at Melody again. "I'm going to tell you what turned my life around, but I'm going to let Annie tell you her own story. I think that's the fair thing to do."

"Did you and Annie talk about this?" Melody raised her eyebrows.

"We discussed the fact that I've never volunteered any information about my past. Adam knows, but he's the only one."

Melody leaned forward. "Ian, you don't have to tell me anything if you don't want to."

Ian waved off her suggestion. "I appreciate that, but I think you might as well know my story. Otherwise, you'll always be wondering."

"You're probably right."

"As I mentioned, Annie and I started dating in high school. We went to college in Florida to get away from our parents. We studied hard during the week, but we partied harder on the weekends. A pattern we established in high school although to a lesser extent."

Melody frowned. "And your parents had no clue?"

"I'm sure if they had, my dad would've put an end to it, but both sets of parents were too busy with their own pursuits to notice."

"Did your parents approve of your relationship with Annie?"

"Yeah. My parents loved Annie. They thought two *good* Christian kids were right for each other. They never imagined what we were doing."

"They never questioned anything?"

Ian shrugged. "*How was your date with Annie?* That's about the extent of it.

"After college graduation we both got good jobs in Orlando. When we eloped without telling our parents, they weren't very happy, but we didn't care. We were living the high life. At least that's what we thought."

"What happened?"

"About six months after we were married, I had a business meeting one night and had a lot to drink. No one was keeping track, or they wouldn't have let me drive home. I could hold my liquor and didn't appear to be drunk, but I was. Way over the limit."

"So you drove drunk?"

Ian nodded. "Not something I like to admit. Thankfully, I was the only one involved in the accident. On the way home, I was going too fast and failed to negotiate a curve. I slammed into a tree on a remote road. Someone finally drove by and saw my car lights in the woods. Somehow I managed to survive, and the accident served as a wake-up call."

"Did your parents finally know how you'd been living?"

"Yeah, I confessed everything, expecting my dad to blow through the roof, but instead, he actually cried. He prayed for me and took time off from his pulpit. He stayed in Orlando until I'd recovered enough to go back to Atlanta at his insistence."

"What about Annie? Where was she during all this?"

"I think the whole episode scared her, too. She was there for me. She quit partying on the weekends with our friends and moved back to Atlanta with me and got a good job. She helped me while I was going through the grueling physical therapy. She couldn't have been more supportive."

Melody's brow wrinkled. "So how did everything fall apart, or is this the part you don't want to talk about?"

"I feel responsible for her not staying sober."

"Why?

"When I fully recovered, I decided to go to law school. My parents encouraged it, and even Annie seemed to think it was a good idea and said we could live on her salary. We even started going to church together."

"Sounds like things were going well."

Ian stared at the floor, then finally looked up. "Yeah, for a while. I think my going back to school was partly to blame for Annie falling back into her old ways. Those first few months of law school, I spent a lot of time studying with my study group. Annie was at loose ends and started going out with her coworkers after work. Pretty soon she was drinking again, but I wasn't paying attention to her activities."

"You can't blame yourself for what she did. She made her own decisions."

"I know, but if I'd paid more attention to my wife, things might have been different."

Melody shook her head. "You don't know that. How do you feel about Annie being here?"

Ian wondered how he could explain the emotions he was feeling. He didn't want to reveal the hurt, the humiliation or the sense of failure Annie's presence produced. "Let's just say it's complicated. I want to help her, but her broken promises over the years don't inspire my trust."

"I'm beginning to see a lot of things." Melody

scooted forward in her chair. "After hearing about your relationship with Annie, I know this is a lot to ask, but I still think we need to give her a chance to prove herself."

"With our finances?"

"Yes. I believe it will give her a sense of purpose and help with her recovery."

Ian gritted his teeth as he got up and walked over to his office window and looked out at this place he loved. Could Annie's financial knowledge help save The Village, or would it only lead to more trouble? What a miserable set of circumstances he faced in an effort to put this ministry on a solid footing—dealing with his father and his ex-wife. Ian turned back to Melody. "You know I'll do just about anything to keep The Village going. So I'll go along with your suggestion about Annie, but you can believe I'll be watching her every move."

Chapter Three

The quiet of the massive church auditorium enveloped Ian as he walked down the carpeted aisle, his footsteps barely making a sound. The plush stadium seats reminded him of a theater. Thousands came to worship here each Sunday and hear his dad preach. Many people had come to know the Lord through this church, but Ian had never felt at home here while he was growing up. He wished he had. Then maybe he and Annie wouldn't have drifted away from the church and wound up living ungodly lives.

As a preacher's kid, he should've been someone who led her away from the devastating behavior, but instead, he had joined her—both of them trying to escape the unhappiness with their family situations. She didn't think her family cared about her, because her parents were too consumed with their jobs and were never home. He, on the other hand, hated being a preacher's kid because everyone expected him to be faultless, like his two older brothers.

Ian found the perfect companion in Annie. They shared a feeling of disinterest from their parents and siblings. Annie's solution was to engage in risky activities. Ian had loved her as much as a sixteen-year-old boy could love a girl, and he feared losing her love if he tried to persuade her not to do those things. Maybe he could've saved her from self-destruction, but he never tried. Instead, he had joined her, and eventually they'd brought each other down.

Annie's reappearance brought back all those guilty feelings. She seemed to be on his mind at every turn. Maybe after he got her connected with another attorney and let his dad know that she was at The Village, he could quit thinking about her.

Every Friday Ian and his dad had a lunch meeting. They'd been doing this ever since Ian had finished law school. He liked meeting with his dad, but Ian always wondered whether getting together was just an excuse for his dad to make sure Ian hadn't fallen off the wagon. He could never quite shake the idea that he still hadn't won his dad's approval even after all this time.

The suspicions were groundless, but they remained in the back of Ian's mind like pesky dandelions that reappeared in the lawn every spring.

During these lunches, he kept the conversation light because he wanted to avoid subjects where there was a clear disagreement. But today's lunch would force him to discuss two of those subjects—Annie and The Village.

Ian usually went straight to his dad's office, but today he'd chosen to walk through the auditorium. He wasn't sure why, but despite the immensity of the place, it offered a place of solitude where he could figure out how he was going to tell his dad about Annie.

After all, his dad was the one who had suggested giving Annie the ultimatum that made her leave. How many times had Ian wished he hadn't told her that she had to quit drinking or move out? She'd packed her bags right then and there. He had always regretted the decision to follow his dad's advice. Annie might not have left if he'd tried to help her more.

Ian sighed. He sank into one of the chairs in the rows near the front. Putting his head in his hands, he began to pray for Annie. Pray for his dad. Pray for himself. *Lord, help me find my way. Please give me the guidance and wisdom I need with my dad and Annie.*

"Ian." The sound of Jordan Montgomery's voice echoed through the auditorium.

Ian scrambled to his feet. "Dad, what are you doing here?"

"I came looking for you. I saw your car in the parking lot and wondered where you were." Jordan knit his eyebrows together above his gray eyes so similar to his own. "What are *you* doing in here?"

Ian lowered his gaze. What should he say to his dad? The truth might be a good idea. Taking a deep breath, Ian looked up at his dad. "I came here to pray."

Jordan smiled. "That's good to hear. Would you like to share your prayers with me, so I can pray for those things, too?"

"Let's go to lunch. We can talk about them over our meal." Ian turned toward the door. "I can drive."

"Okay. I've got to grab a few things from my office before we go. I'll be out in a minute."

Ian wasted no time getting to his car. He got inside and pressed the buttons to lower the windows. While he waited for his dad, he figured he had a few more minutes to pray, but he barely had time to get into his vehicle before his dad appeared. "That was quick."

Jordan chuckled. "I may be getting old, son, but I'm not that slow. Where are we headed today?"

"How about that mom-and-pop place just down the road?" His dad was still young at fifty-eight. He had a little gray hair at the temples and a few more smile lines than he used to have, but he could easily be mistaken for a man at least a decade younger. Folks were often surprised to know that Jordan had a son Ian's age and even more surprised that he had two older brothers. "Suits me. I had a light breakfast, so I'm hungry and ready for lunch."

Ian didn't say a thing. He usually would have agreed, but today his stomach was tied in knots. He wasn't sure how much he could eat. With the hope of limiting any conversation, he turned on the radio, tuned to a Christian music station. That did the trick. His dad started singing along.

When they reached the restaurant, they walked in silence across the parking lot. Inside the hostess led them to a corner table covered with a red-and-white-checked tablecloth and laid the menus on the table. Ian settled on the Windsor chair and picked up a menu. He looked it over, but all the choices swam before his eyes. He couldn't focus because thoughts of Annie consumed his mind. The waitress took their drink orders and returned momentarily with them and took their meal orders.

Crossing his arms, Jordan sat back in the chair. "Are you ready to tell me what you were praying about?"

"Not really, but I suppose it has to be done." Ian wondered whether he should start with Annie or the budget crisis at The Village. Neither topic was something he wanted to mention, but he wished to talk about Annie the least.

A frown furrowed Jordan's brow. "Have you fallen off the wagon?"

Ian laughed halfheartedly and shook his head. "No, Dad, nothing like that. I need to talk to you about what happened at the board meeting on Monday."

Jordan grimaced. "Sorry I asked that question. I should've known better."

Ian hated that his dad had asked that question, but he understood his father's rationale. He'd missed the signs of substance abuse before, and he wasn't going to do it again. "I don't fault you for asking. My former addictions are something I'll always have to live with."

"So what happened at the board meeting?"

"The board is threatening to close The Village because donations are down and the financial situation is critical. You know how much that place does for people and how much it means to me." Ian gave his dad a recap of the board meeting.

"So they asked you to tap us for more money?"

"Yeah. I know you already give, but is there any way you could see clear to increase the amount and have the congregation become more of a partner with The Village?"

Jordan steepled his fingers under his chin as he continued to lean back in his chair, his elbows on the armrests. "You know we've had our disagreements over the years about your work there, and we usually steer clear of the subject."

"Yeah." Ian prepared himself for a lecture from

his dad on how giving money to The Village was to spend more money on something that ultimately would never succeed. His dad was probably going to say he agreed with Bob Franklin.

"You know that it isn't really up to me. The church elders are the ones who allocate where money goes, but I can certainly call for more volunteers."

"You will?"

Frowning, Jordan nodded. "Why does that surprise you?"

"I thought you weren't sold on what we do at The Village."

Jordan nodded. "In the beginning, I was skeptical that the concept would work, but I've had a change of heart. I've seen what you do and how much the center helps people."

"Why didn't you ever tell me?"

Jordan shrugged. "I thought the fact that my congregation agreed to support the work spoke for itself. Guess you needed to hear that."

Ian nodded, realizing God had affirmatively answered one of his prayers. He hoped that boded well for his prayers concerning Annie. "What do you suggest I do to gain more support from your congregation?"

"Talk to the elders."

"Really?" Ian would rather stand in front of a judge and jury. They might cut him more slack than the elders of this church. His past behavior hadn't made him any friends on the church board.

Jordan nodded. "I believe you're capable of persuading them. After all, you're a lawyer and good one at that. Plead your case."

Before Ian could respond to his dad's praise and pep talk, the waitress brought their food. Jordan said a prayer, and then they ate in silence for several minutes. The whole time Ian's thoughts were centered on Annie. Telling his dad about her was his next big hurdle.

Jordan took a gulp of water, then looked at Ian. "Would you like me to put you on the agenda for the next board meeting?"

"If that's what it'll take."

"I have confidence in you, son. They know you're a good man."

Ian tried to keep the surprise off his face. "I thought they didn't think much of me because of my former behavior."

"Not so anymore. They've seen how you've turned your life around."

"They don't mind that I don't attend your church?"

Jordan shrugged. "Why should they? They know you work at The Village. It only makes sense that you would attend church there."

"That's good to know." Ian could hardly believe how this conversation was working out. Even though he'd been having a lunch meeting with his dad every Friday for years, they'd never talked like this. Why had he doubted God could turn what Ian had termed a difficult conversation into a conversation that enhanced his relationship with his father? This outcome gave Ian the courage to talk about Annie.

"Then I'll put you on the agenda for next week's meeting." Jordan took another bite of his sandwich.

Ian took a drink of water, then cleared his throat. "There's something else I need to tell you about The Village."

"You're dating that pretty blonde who heads the women's ministry."

Ian chuckled. "No, Dad, but it does involve a woman. Annie."

Jordan put down his sandwich and stared at Ian. "Annie? What does she have to do with The Village?"

Trying not to convey any emotion, Ian quickly recounted how Annie had come to be there. Then he held his breath as he waited for a response. Ian had no idea what his dad thought about her these days.

"You didn't say how you're feeling about Annie's presence there."

So his dad wasn't going to say what he thought about Annie. Instead, he turned the question on Ian. "It hasn't been easy. That's what I've been praying about. Since she's shown up, I've had to tell Melody about my past. At least, I haven't had to explain to anyone else."

"What did Melody say?"

"She was surprised. That's all. But she thinks Annie can help us with the funding crisis because of her financial consulting background."

"And you don't?" Jordan narrowed his gaze.

"I have my reservations."

"Why?"

Ian wasn't sure he wanted to denigrate Annie's image any further. Besides, the whole episode that sparked the deep distrust would make him look as bad as Annie. It was better left untold. "At this early stage in her residence at The Village, how can any of us really trust her? She's been unreliable in the past. How can we begin to give her access to the financial dealings of The Village?"

Jordan wrinkled his brow as he raised his eyebrows. "I can't answer that question. Sometimes, you have to step out in faith. Have faith that God will help Annie stay sober."

Ian slowly shook his head. "The last time I saw Annie before she showed up at The Village she only wanted to use me. After that, I didn't ever want to see her again."

"Is that how you still feel today?"

"She's a chapter in my life I'd like to forget. Now I can't." Even as Ian said the words, he wondered whether he was being completely honest with himself. He certainly wanted her to find her way to a substance-free life. He wanted her to succeed in every way. On a personal level, he couldn't decipher his feelings.

"I'm sure this has disrupted your life, but I believe the Lord will use this for your benefit."

"I wish I could see how."

"You will." Jordan cleared his throat. "I think Melody has an excellent idea about using Annie's knowledge of finances to help The Village."

"I can't trust her."

"Pray about it. I've been praying for Annie every day since your divorce. She and I became very close while you were recovering from your accident. It broke my heart to see her slip back into her old ways." Jordan's voice cracked.

Ian knew little about his dad's real feelings. He'd refused to discuss these kinds of issues with the man for years because Ian feared disapproval. "How come we've never talked like this before?"

"I sensed that you didn't want to discuss Annie. You were hurting, and I didn't want to make you feel worse. I love you both." Jordan nodded.

Ian wondered about his dad's statement. "If you loved us, why did you suggest I give her that ultimatum?"

Jordan lowered his head and didn't say anything

for a moment. When he finally met Ian's gaze, Ian saw the sorrow in his dad's eyes. "At the time, I thought it was the best thing to do. I thought it would give her a wake-up call, but I was wrong. I didn't mean to cause you hurt, but I didn't think things could go on the way they were."

Ian wasn't sure what to say. They couldn't go back and change things. They just had to move forward.

"The news that Annie is making a go of it does my heart good, and I'll put in a good word to the board about more funding for this ministry. I want to see Annie and *you* succeed."

"Thanks, Dad."

"And maybe this opening with Annie will lead to bringing her family back into the church. You know they left after your divorce."

"Annie told me she hasn't seen them in three years. She said they didn't want anything to do with her."

"I wondered what happened with her parents. They showed up one day out of the blue about three years ago and blamed you and me and the church for Annie's demise."

"What'd you do?" Ian wondered why his dad had never said anything. Probably the same reason they'd never talked about Annie. His dad was trying to protect him. Today's conversation put a whole new light on his relationship with his father.

Jordan grimaced. "I sat there and took their accusations. There wasn't much sense in arguing with them. They said their piece, then left. I've been praying for them, too. So maybe you can talk to Annie about trying to reconcile with her parents."

"Dad, I don't think we can dump this much stuff on her all at once."

"You're probably right, but when you get a chance bring it up casually."

"Go slow, Dad. Don't rush her."

Jordan grinned. "You still care about her."

Ian shook his head. "Don't get any ideas about me and her. Our relationship is history—ancient history."

"Okay. I get the message, but I'll be praying for you." Jordan held up one hand. "I have one request. Instead of our lunch meeting next Friday, I want you to bring Annie to dinner at the house."

Ian's heart sank as he swallowed a huge lump in his throat. Was that really a good idea, but how could he refuse his father's request. "What if she doesn't want to come?"

"If you ask, I think she'll come." Standing, Jordan picked up the bill from the table. "I've got it today."

"Okay. Thanks again." Ian wasn't sure whether he wanted his dad to be right or wrong about Annie accepting the invitation.

* * *

Almost two weeks had gone by since Annie had arrived at The Village. She'd already had her first job interview, and she could hardly wait to talk to Melody about it. All had gone well, but Annie didn't want to be overconfident. Sunlight glinted off the windows as she approached the administration building. The trill of a robin's call sounded from a nearby tree. The beautiful weather and surroundings put a spring in her step. Her excitement bubbled over as she entered the front door.

"Good morning, Lovie."

"Good morning to you, too. You sound chipper." Lovie smiled. "Your interview must have gone well."

"It did." Annie knit her eyebrows. "How did you know about my interview?"

Lovie wagged a finger at Annie. "There's not much that goes on around this place that I don't know about."

"I'll have to remember that you're keeping tabs on everyone."

"You might say that." Lovie grinned. "Are you settling in okay—meeting lots of people?"

Annie stepped up to the counter. "I've met so many people. I'm beginning to lose track of everyone's name. We should all be required to wear name tags like you."

Lovie glanced down and rubbed a finger across

the little gold bar pinned to her blouse that sported her name. "Well, you'll never forget who I am."

Annie chuckled. "Lovie, you're the best. You always make me smile."

"Now don't go braggin' on me. I might get a big head." Lovie patted her silver hair. "Who are you here to see?"

"Melody and Ian."

"The dynamic duo. Those two are the busiest people I've ever known. You best be on your way." Lovie waved in the direction of Melody's office. "Have a good meeting."

"Thanks." Annie shuffled down the hallway, nerves increasing the closer she got to the office. She didn't mind meeting with Melody and wanted to share her news with her. Meeting with Ian was a different matter. His presence would make her nervous and uncertain. Annie knocked on the office door and, in a second, Melody opened it and ushered Annie inside. "How did your interview go?"

Annie glanced around. Ian wasn't there. She wasn't sure whether to be happy or disappointed. Her emotions concerning Ian flitted from wanting him around to hoping she didn't have to deal with him. "I think it went really well. Thanks for the interview practice. I was prepared to answer every question they asked."

"Did they say what the next step would be? A callback interview? What?"

"They said they would get back to me by Friday at the latest, probably sooner. Although I think I did well, I'm glad it's over. I'll be on pins and needles until they call." Annie let out a loud sigh.

"I'm so excited the interview went well." Melody sat on the chair behind her desk. "Have a seat. Ian will be here in a minute."

"Okay." Annie sat on one of the chairs on the other side of the desk from Melody.

"How are you feeling about Ian's presence here? Why didn't you tell me you and Ian had been married?" Leaning forward, Melody clasped her hands on top of her desk.

Annie smiled wryly. "We've spent a lot of time together in the last few days. How come you didn't ask me about it before now?"

"You certainly know how to turn a question around." Melody chuckled. "I kept thinking you'd tell me, but since you didn't I thought before this meeting would be a good time to ask."

"I was pretty sure Ian had told you about us, but I wasn't going to initiate that topic of conversation unless I knew for sure. He had the right not to talk about it if he didn't want to."

"Okay. Back to the original question. How are you dealing with him being here?"

Just as Annie opened her mouth to answer, a knock sounded on the door, and Ian entered the office. "Sorry I'm late. I was trying to confirm things with Scott Bartlett. He'll be here after lunch to talk with Annie."

"Wonderful." Melody motioned for Ian to sit.

"It is." Ian took the chair next to Annie. "Did I miss anything?"

"Annie's good news about her interview."

"Guess we haven't talked since our last meeting." Ian smiled at her. "It must've gone well."

"It did." Annie's stomach somersaulted. Ian had actually smiled at her. She couldn't let that affect her thinking. She wanted him to be happy for her, but she had to keep everything in perspective. Nothing had changed between them. He was only here because Melody had asked him to come. The fact that Ian hadn't spoken to her since the day she'd arrived here told Annie just how little he was thinking of her. Out of sight, out of mind.

"Great." Ian turned his attention to Melody. "Have the two of you talked about Annie helping us here?"

"No, we were talking about her interview. I was waiting for you before I brought it up." Melody pulled a folder from a drawer in her desk, then glanced at Annie. "Ian and I have a request to make of you."

"What?" Annie's voice wavered. What could they possibly want from her?

Melody tapped her fingers on the folder as it lay on the desk. "Since you have financial consulting experience, we were hoping you'd come to our administrative meeting on Monday of next week. We'd like to hear your opinion regarding the financial state of The Village. We're hoping you could help us streamline our operation and show us how we can make better use of our funds as well as finding more ways to raise money."

Annie remembered when a request like this had been a challenge—one she'd accepted with pleasure. She'd been good at helping companies and businesses, especially nonprofits get a handle on their balance sheets. Was she prepared to tackle something like that now?

"I know we've kind of sprung this on you without warning, but we're in need of some advice."

Annie had no idea what to say. They were asking for her advice. They weren't looking at her as a recovering alcoholic or substance abuser. They were looking at her as an equal. Of course, Melody did the talking. Ian sat there taking it all in. Was he on board with this request, or was he only going along to please Melody? What difference did it make? This was a chance to prove herself, especially to Ian. She wanted him to respect her once again, but she had to keep the thought of loving him again far, far away. So why did the idea keep popping into her mind?

"So what do you say?" Melody tilted her head. "Have we scared you off?"

Annie took a deep breath. "I'll sit in on the meeting, but I have to be honest. I don't know whether I can help or not."

Melody nodded. "I understand. I think the more idea people we have reviewing the finances the better off we'll be. Thanks for agreeing to attend."

"Thank you for inviting me." Annie eased back in her chair, the tension draining from her body.

Melody picked up the folder and held it out. "Maybe you'd like to look this over."

Before Annie could take the folder, Ian reached over and snatched it. "I know you have another meeting to go to, so why don't you let me take this down to my office and go over it with Annie? Scott will be coming to my office to meet Annie, anyway."

A strange look passed between Ian and Melody before she finally smiled. "Sure. If that's what you want to do."

"Yeah. That'll work out best." Ian stood and looked down at Annie. "Ready?"

"Okay." Annie stood and turned to Melody. "Thanks again for including me in the project."

Melody walked around her desk and gave Annie a hug. "We're glad to have you. Keep me informed about the job."

"I will. Talk to you later."

"I'll be praying for your upcoming meeting and your job." Melody looked as though she wanted to say something else, but she stood there with what appeared to be a forced smile.

Annie sensed friction between Melody and Ian. The uneasy feeling Annie had experienced earlier returned as she followed Ian to the door. She wished she had more time to spend with Melody, but it wasn't going to happen today.

They'd barely been here ten minutes, and already Ian was rushing off and insisting that she go with him. Understanding dawned. Melody's request was definitely not Ian's idea. He didn't trust her to look over the finances without some supervision. The realization pierced her heart. But could she blame him? She'd stolen from him to fund her drug habit. She would not only have to earn his respect again, but his trust, as well.

Chapter Four

While Annie and Ian walked to his office, he didn't say a thing. He didn't look at her. He didn't even acknowledge her presence. What was he thinking? She probably didn't want to know.

He opened the door and motioned for her to go in, still giving her the silent treatment. If he wanted this meeting, he needed to say something. Even if he didn't trust her, and she had to prove a lot of things to him, she wasn't going to let him treat her like some timid little mouse. She wasn't going to jump when he said jump.

Annie stood in the middle of the room. When he looked at her with those intense gray eyes, her resolve weakened.

"It's okay to sit down." He wasn't ordering her to sit, but it sure seemed like it.

Annie stared at the nearby chair. This was silly. He was only being polite. Why was she making it into something it wasn't? She hated feeling dependent on Ian. For some reason Melody didn't make her feel that way, even though Annie depended on Melody for all kinds of help. Maybe it was the sisterly relationship that had developed in the short time she'd been at The Village.

Annie finally settled on the chair. "I thought you said the other attorney wasn't coming until after lunch. What are we doing in the meantime?"

Ian put the folder on his desk, but he didn't sit in the chair behind his desk as Annie thought he would. Instead, he sat in the chair next to hers and turned it until he was facing hers. "We've got some things to discuss."

"What things?" Annie swallowed a lump in her throat as she also turned her chair until they were sitting face-to-face. Was he going to bring up her long-ago transgressions?

Ian stared at the floor as if he was gathering his thoughts. When he looked up, the uncertainty in his eyes surprised her. That was not the Ian she had always known. He'd been confident, sometimes even cocky. He'd known what he wanted, and he went after it. She'd always liked that about him.

"I had a meeting with my dad last Friday, and I told him you were here."

Oh, great. Annie wondered whether Ian's dad had given him another ultimatum to pass on to her.

During Ian's recovery from his accident, Annie had actually felt close to Jordan Montgomery. He seemed to care about her, but she'd come to believe it was an act. Annie stared at Ian. Did he want some kind of reaction from her? What was she supposed to say?

"Annie, are you afraid of what I'm going to say?"

Was she? "I don't know. This whole situation with you and me is very awkward."

Ian smiled wryly. His shoulders relaxed as he settled back in his chair. "That's for sure. I feel like I've been walking through a minefield since you got here."

Ian's honesty surprised Annie. "That pretty much describes the situation. So what did your dad say?"

"He thinks Melody's idea to have you on the finances team is a good one."

If Annie hadn't been gripping the armrest of her chair, she would have fallen out of it. Her mouth hanging open, she stared at Ian. She shook her head to make sure she wasn't dreaming. "He really said that?"

"He did."

"But you have your reservations, right?"

"I can't say that I don't, and I'm sure you know why."

Annie nodded. "But I'm not that person anymore."

"I'd like to believe that, but I trusted you before, and you let me down."

Annie hung her head. That was the awful truth. Feeling his scrutiny, she finally looked up. "I did. More times than I want to admit, but this time I'm going to get it right. If I don't, I'll lose my kids forever. I can't let that happen."

"I'll be with you every step of the way if you show me you've changed for good."

"I'll show you." Her heart raced while she returned Ian's gaze. She wouldn't look away or let him intimidate her. But she certainly couldn't let him know how he made her feel—that after all this time he still made her heart race when she looked at him. How could she ever show him that she was different without letting him see those feelings?

"Good." Ian reached over and retrieved the folder from his desk. "We can go over this in a minute, but first I want to tell you what else my dad said."

"Okay." Annie braced herself for the worst as Ian started to talk.

"Besides his agreement with Melody, he wants me to bring you to dinner Friday night."

"Dinner?"

"Yeah, you know that evening meal."

Annie let out an exasperated sigh. "I know what you mean, but I don't believe this."

"Surprised me, too."

"I suppose I should go." Annie narrowed her gaze. "So how do you feel about having me inflicted on you from multiple corners?"

"You should, and I'll live." Ian gave her a wry smile and got up to sit behind his desk. "Now let's go over the stuff in this folder."

"Sure." As Annie scooted her chair closer to his desk, she didn't know what to make of the dinner invitation or Ian's willingness to issue the invitation or the fact that he hadn't disputed her question about being plagued with her presence. She couldn't dwell on it, or these thoughts would drive her crazy. Everything about the situation with Ian gave her conflicting messages.

Her emotions.

His reactions.

Any idea that even hinted at reconciliation with Ian was lunacy. She had to quit hoping for the impossible.

Ian opened the folder, his strong hand resting on the pages inside. After a momentary hesitation, he shoved the folder at her. "Here. Take a look."

Annie took the pages and leafed through them. The situation here at The Village became quite clear. This ministry was in financial trouble. The expenditures far exceeded the income. How could she possibly help? What would happen to her if this place suddenly closed its doors? Everything she wanted depended on this place.

Annie looked up. "You need more than my help. You need a miracle worker."

Ian nodded. "We have one. We just have to let Him work."

"Faith. I'm still working on that."

"Me, too, actually."

Annie didn't know what to think of Ian's admission. Was he only trying to make her feel better because her faith was a work in progress? She had to quit trying to decipher his motives. She should concentrate on the pages in front of her. "Can you tell me what's been happening here?"

"Bottom line. Donations have slowed to a trickle. We still have most of the churches that support us on a regular basis, but we're way down on individual donations. Many children's sponsors, who are usually individuals, have dropped their sponsorships."

"Have you done any belt-tightening?"

Ian nodded. "No salary increases. If someone left, we didn't replace them. Double duty for a lot of us. We wear multiple hats. Melody is in charge of the women's ministry and the children's ministry. I take care of the legal parts of the ministry and oversee the assisted-living facility and nursing center. It seems to me that we've cut to the bone, but maybe you can see something we don't. We definitely need more funds. How do we get those?"

How many times had she heard that same question when she'd been working with a nonprofit entity? The answer was never easy. Annie stared at the pages in her hands, afraid to look at Ian. "I can't help you unless I can take this information and study it. You seem intent on making sure I have supervision while I do it."

"Annie, I—"

She looked up. "You don't have to make excuses."

Ian cleared his throat. "I was going to apologize for treating you like you have a sinister agenda."

"Do you really mean that?" When Ian hesitated Annie's heart sank. He couldn't give her a straight-out yes. "So you don't."

"You're putting words in my mouth."

Annie sighed. "You didn't have any words of your own, so what am I to think?"

"I want to believe I can trust you, but a part of me remembers…"

He remembered the bad stuff she'd done—the way she'd hurt him, the way she'd let him down, the way she'd traded his love for drugs and booze. The same old things continued to create a gulf between them. Maybe Melody was treating her as an equal, but Ian wasn't. Could he ever put those things behind him? She blinked hard and pressed her lips together as tears threatened. She wasn't going to let him make her cry.

Strong. She had to be strong. She closed her eyes for a moment. Faith. This is where she needed faith—faith that God would see her through this. She had to rely on God's strength, not her own.

"Annie."

Hearing the sorrow in Ian's voice, she opened her eyes. He'd come around to the front of the desk and sat on the edge very near her chair.

Her smile wavered, but she looked him right in the eyes. "Yes."

"You can have the papers to study. But bring them to the meeting next Monday."

"Where and what time?"

"Adam's office. Eight o'clock."

"Thank you."

Ian picked up his cell phone from the desk. "It's almost noon. Want to go to lunch with me before we meet with Scott?"

Another shocker. Ian was volunteering to be with her. Was this good or bad? "Sure."

"Great. I'm headed over to the assisted-living facility."

Annie smiled. "That'll give me a chance to see Cora."

"Absolutely." Ian escorted Annie to the door.

While they walked across campus, birds chirped in the trees. A rainbow of tulips surrounded the fountain in the middle of the quad. The smell of newly mowed grass filled the air. Annie took in the sights, sounds and smells with a new appreciation for God's creation. For too many years her mind had been in a fog. Nothing would take her back to that time. Absolutely nothing.

Annie glanced over at Ian. He was reading something on his cell phone. She didn't even mind that he wasn't paying attention to her. He'd invited her to lunch of his own accord. She would savor this time with him and figure out where he fit into her life later.

While Ian walked beside Annie, he scrolled through the email on his cell phone. The distraction was easier than trying to figure out what to say to her. What had possessed him to invite her to lunch? Maybe the fact that he'd almost made her cry.

What a bully. What could she do with the papers? Nothing. She'd paid for her sins with the loss of her children. Whatever the circumstances, he had a soft spot for Annie. Always had. That's how they'd started dating. He saw how much the death of her grandparents had affected her. They'd paid attention to her while her parents left her without any guidance. Then he'd contributed to her drift by joining in her rebellious behavior. He wanted to do whatever he could to make things right for her, but he feared that soft spot might turn into something more than he wanted.

"I hope you don't spend the entire lunch glued to your phone."

Ian glanced over at Annie. She was grinning, so he guessed he wasn't in too much trouble.

Sometimes she seemed to be the Annie he used to know—the one from the early days of their marriage when they used to have fun together—before the weekend drinking binges became a part of their weekday life. "So you want to talk to me? I thought you were going to spend your time talking with Cora and her friends."

"Don't you want to join in our conversation? It'll be you and a group of beautiful women. What more could a guy ask for?"

"Not much." Ian pocketed his phone as he gazed at Annie. Beautiful. That described her.

"Thank you."

"For putting my phone away?"

"Yeah. And for trusting me enough to give me the financial reports."

"Don't thank me for those. They're a nightmare."

Annie sighed. "We can tackle this. You said we have a miracle worker on our side. He worked a miracle with me."

Ian wanted to believe Annie's statement. He should have faith that God had truly changed Annie's life and would continue to work in her life. He opened the door to the assisted-living center. "We have to sign in at the reception desk."

"Even you?"

"Everyone. It's the policy. The staff wants to account for everyone who's in the building."

"I can understand that where I live in the women's shelter, but why here?"

"Safety first everywhere on campus." Ian signed his name, then handed the pen to Annie. Their fingers brushed, and he nearly dropped the pen. He wasn't prepared for his reaction to her touch. This couldn't be good, not mixed with all the other thoughts he'd had this morning. She hadn't been here very long, and already she'd insinuated herself into his life. Where was he going to find safety for his heart?

After Annie signed in, she turned to him. "I guess that's why you have the guard and gates at the entrance."

Ian nodded. "Sounds like you've talked to some of the women who live in your building?"

"Yeah."

Ian wondered whether the bum who'd fathered Annie's children had ever abused her. He hoped not, but he couldn't ask that question. If she wanted him to know, she would volunteer the information. Did she still love the man? The thought curdled Ian's stomach. Why had he let his mind wander down that road?

Ian pointed straight ahead. "The dining room is through those double doors. Something on the menu smells good."

Annie grinned. "It does."

Ian ushered her through the line as they both

took the fried chicken, mashed potatoes and gravy, along with a helping of green beans. Ian glanced around the room until he spotted Cora and her friends. They occupied half of a round table that seated six people. "Cora, Liz and Ruby are over there."

"Looks like they have room at their table." Annie headed that way.

"Would you like me to get you a drink?" Ian called after her.

Annie turned, a smile on her face. "Please. Some sweet tea."

"You've got it." Ian headed for the drink station, thinking that he should have remembered Annie liked sweet tea. Of course, he also remembered that she'd liked rum and Coke, more often than not. He pushed the thought away, not wanting to think about the bad parts of Annie's life. He should think on the good things, but the good things got him into trouble. They made him wonder whether… No he wouldn't go there. Today was the only thing he should consider. He couldn't speculate about the future where Annie was concerned. He put two iced teas on his tray and made his way to the table where Annie was already engaged in conversation with the three older ladies.

Ian looked over the group. "May I join you?"

Cora chuckled. "Of course. Annie told us a handsome man was coming to our table."

A pink blush tinged Annie's cheeks as she looked up at him. "Don't believe a word she says unless she tells you she's the one who called you handsome."

Trying not to smile, Ian emptied his tray and picked up Annie's. "I'll get rid of these. No talking about me while I'm gone."

"Your ears will be burning." Cora laughed.

As Ian walked away, he was thankful that three elderly ladies would serve as a buffer between him and his runaway thoughts about Annie. When he returned, Annie, who was sitting next to Cora, stared up at him. "I waited to eat until you got back, so you could say a blessing for the food."

"Sure." Ian sat on the chair next to Annie and bowed his head. He needed to pray for more than the food. He needed wisdom for this whole situation, but he certainly wasn't going to voice that prayer aloud.

During their lunch, Ian mostly listened while the ladies talked. The older ladies told Annie about their grandchildren, and she talked about Kara and Spencer. He hoped one day she could be with her children again.

Cora looked his way. "Ian, you're quiet today. What's on your mind?"

Annie, but he wasn't going to say so. "Too many things to list. We've got a lot going on here."

"Are you helping this young lady reunite with her children?" Liz gave him a pointed look.

Annie nodded. "He is. I just want to get the process started."

Ian grabbed his phone from his pocket and looked at the time. "And you're going to do that in a few minutes. We need to head back to my office."

"I'm ready." Annie hopped up from her chair.

"You two run along. Ruby, Liz and I will take care of your plates." Cora shooed them away with a wave of her hand. "We'll be praying for you, too."

"Thanks." Annie went around the table and gave each of the ladies a hug. "One can never have enough prayers. Bye."

As they walked out of the dining room, Ian knew it was good for Annie to make friends. She needed all the support she could get. But after spending his lunch with her, he would be glad to hand her off to Scott Bartlett. For his own peace of mind, they couldn't part company soon enough.

"Do you attend your dad's church?" Annie's question came out of the blue.

Ian wondered what had prompted her inquiry. "No."

"Where do you go?"

Why was she concerned about where he went to church? "I attend here on campus."

"I didn't see you on Sunday."

"So you were looking for me?" Was she looking for him because she wanted to see him or avoid him?

"I was just curious." Annie gave him a sideways glance. "You know, I'm a different person. Faith in Jesus has completely changed my life. I want you to know that."

Ian puzzled over Annie's declaration about church and her faith. Was she trying to reassure him ahead of this meeting that she was ready and deserving of having her children back? He wished he could let go of his doubts, but they hung there in his mind like rotted curtains at a window. They reminded him of the dismal state she'd come from and her numerous relapses. "I have to be honest, Annie. I'm still skeptical. I don't doubt you have good intentions. I just need to *see* you carry them out."

Her eyes blinked rapidly as her lips quivered. She didn't say anything until they reached the fountain. She stopped in front of it. Water spilled from level to level, sparkling in the sunlight. "I know I have a lot to prove. Do I have time to stop at my apartment before the meeting?"

Ian checked the time on his phone. "Yeah, but don't be late."

"I won't be." Annie sprinted across the quad as if something were chasing her.

Glued to the spot, Ian watched her until she disappeared inside her building. He'd done it again—almost made her cry. Why had he been so blunt with her? Being honest with her made both of them unhappy, but he couldn't sugarcoat what he thought. She would either prove herself or not. He should be more supportive, but he knew the pitfalls of recovery. None of it was easy. He'd been through it himself.

Should he be more sympathetic? No. Annie didn't need sympathy. She needed support that was straightforward. He would give her that and nothing more.

Annie couldn't reach her apartment fast enough. She sniffled as she ran across the expansive lawn. Tears blurred her vision as she struggled to punch in the code to gain entrance to the building. She fumbled with the key to open her door. Once inside she flung herself onto the sofa and laid her head back. She had to pull herself together before the meeting with this lawyer. She wanted to be strong, but Ian's doubts hurt her deep down inside. Her heart ached, but she couldn't wallow in self-pity.

Sitting up, she took a deep breath. She wanted Ian's approval, but she couldn't dwell on something she might never attain. Not because she couldn't stay clean, but because he couldn't see beyond the woman he used to know.

Annie's disposable cell phone buzzed as it sat

on the coffee table. She recognized the number on the display as belonging to the company where she'd had her interview. She pressed the key to answer the call, her heart racing. "Hello, this is Annie Payton."

"Annie, this is Myra, Mr. Reed's assistant. He wanted me to let you know that they have decided to hire someone else for the position."

Annie's heart sank. She'd been so hopeful. The interview had seemed to go so well. How had she been so wrong? They certainly hadn't wasted any time making a decision. She had to remember that the person they hired probably didn't have an addiction problem in their past. "Oh, okay. Thanks for letting me know."

Annie sank back on the sofa and covered her face with her hands. How was she ever going to get Kara and Spencer back if she couldn't find a job? What would Melody say? What would Ian say? Annie didn't want to cry again, but this news, on top of Ian's negativity, made the tears come, anyway. Sniffling some more, she wiped at her eyes, then pressed a hand to her mouth to stifle the sob that rose from deep in her chest. She couldn't sit here and cry. She had to get to that meeting.

Grabbing a tissue, she wiped the tears from her face. She stuck the phone in her purse and headed out of her apartment. Would Ian notice that she'd been crying? She hoped not. She didn't want him to know that she hadn't gotten the job. Locking the door, she let out a heavy sigh. He would eventually find out, but for now he didn't need to know.

When Annie reached the administration building, she went in the side door closest to Ian's office. She wanted to avoid Lovie because the woman seemed to read people like a book. She would know that all wasn't right. Annie knocked on Ian's door. He opened it immediately, as if he'd been standing right beside it.

"Good, you made it here before Scott arrived. I certainly didn't want you to be late." Ian strode to his desk and busied himself with some paperwork, almost ignoring her presence.

Fuming inside, Annie didn't say anything as she quickly occupied one of the chairs in front of the desk. His statement still ringing in her mind, she tamped down her irritation. He must still think she was irresponsible. She would show him. He'd be sorry he ever doubted her. She took a calming breath. She was jumping to all sorts of conclusions and assigning her own interpretation to his words. She couldn't read his mind.

Annie closed her eyes and took another calming breath. *Lord, help me through this meeting and help me not to clash with Ian.* Just as she opened her eyes, a knock sounded on the door. Ian hurried to open it.

He shook hands with a tall, husky man. The

man's dark brown hair reminded Annie of the hairstyle her father had worn the last time she'd seen him. In fact, other than being tall, the man resembled her father a great deal. How was that going to work out? She didn't want to be reminded of her father every time she met with her lawyer. Could anything else go wrong today?

Ian introduced them, and Annie labored to produce a smile. His beefy hand closed around Annie's as they shook hands. His brown eyes twinkled. A smile lit up his face, and relief filled her mind, putting her at ease. Her confidence rose as she returned to her seat. Today was going to be okay, after all.

Scott glanced around the room. "Where would you like us to work?"

Ian motioned toward his desk. "You can work here, and I'll take my work to the library."

Scott's brow wrinkled. "No need for you to leave. In fact, I'd like for you to sit in on our conversation. I may ask for your input."

"Sure." Ian resumed his seat behind his desk. "Let me know if there's anything you need."

Annie forced herself not to frown as she returned to the chair she'd occupied before Scott had arrived. So maybe today wasn't going to be okay. Why did Ian have to be here if he wasn't going to represent her, especially if he really didn't want to be here? She took another deep breath. If she had to keep calming herself, she might hyperventilate. That would only add to the disaster this day had become.

Scott settled his large frame into the chair opposite Annie. "Ian has filled me in on some of your background, but I want to ask some questions to clarify the things I already know."

"Sure." Annie tried to put her nerves aside by reminding herself that Scott was here to help her.

Scott smiled and asked the first question, which he followed with several more. He scribbled notes as she answered. She wondered what he was writing. What was important to her case? Did she dare ask? No. She didn't want to say the wrong thing or ask a stupid question, especially with Ian listening to the conversation, although he didn't appear to be very interested. Maybe because he knew everything she was going to say. He knew her case. He knew her. And he knew she'd messed up too many times.

Scott looked up from his notes and tapped his pen—something he did when he appeared to be thinking. "Do I understand you to say that you've been substance free for a year, and yet DFCS will not reunite you with your children?"

Annie nodded. "My caseworker says I haven't proven that I can stay clean in an unstructured environment, and I'm a little worried that she may not consider The Village an unstructured environment, either."

"Are you free to come and go here?" Scott continued to tap his pen.

"Yes." Even though she'd answered affirmatively, her life here was sheltered. She had to admit she liked it that way. Her ill-fated job interview and one trip to the nearby strip mall had been her only excursions off campus since she'd arrived.

"Then they can't say you're living in a place like the rehab center where you weren't free to come and go as you please." Scott scribbled a few more notes, then looked up at her. "I'm going to file a motion asking that custody of your children be given back to you."

"How long before we go to court?"

"That depends on the court docket. I'll let you know as soon as I find out." Scott looked over at Ian. "Will you testify on her behalf?"

"Melody will. I'm staying out of it. That's why I asked you to handle the case." Ian kept his eyes trained on Scott.

Annie looked at Ian's nervous expression. He'd never told Scott about their marriage. "I agree with Ian. He should stay out of it."

Scott looked puzzled as he shrugged. "If that's the way you guys want it."

"We do," Annie and Ian answered in chorus.

"One more thing." Scott nodded at Annie. "Melody tells me that you've had a job interview. It would certainly help your case if you have a job by the time we go to court."

Annie's heart sank. Her failed interview was something she didn't want to discuss, but was it wise to keep it to herself? She'd have to tell Melody sometime soon. Annie tried to tell herself another job would come along. "I'm working on it."

"Good. Let me know when you've got a job."

"I certainly will." After the bad news this morning, she didn't have a good feeling about her prospects. Jobs weren't plentiful, anyway. What could she possibly expect to find with her drug-riddled background? Was there any way to put a happy face on this situation?

Of course there was. She had a lot of people here rooting for her—Melody, Cora and her friends, even Ian. She couldn't let troublesome events derail her determination. God had helped her overcome her substance abuse. He would be there through this trial, too. That's what she had to remember.

Chapter Five

The following evening, Ian walked beside Annie on the stepping stones that led to his parents' front door. Her successful meeting with Scott Bartlett appeared to have buoyed her spirits and put her in a good mood. He wished his mood could match hers. Then maybe he could survive the evening with her and his parents. She was dressed for success in one of the outfits Melody had helped Annie pick out when they had shopped at The Village store. Tonight she reminded him of the confident young woman he'd married, but he didn't want to think about that time—too many memories—good and bad.

Ian rang the bell. The door opened immediately, and Jordan Montgomery ushered them into the front hall. His parents now lived in a modest home—not the bigger, more lavish home they'd occupied when he and his two older brothers were all living at home. They'd downsized as soon as Ian had gone to college. He actually liked this smaller place better. It felt more like home even though he'd never lived here.

"Good to see you, Dad." Ian shook his dad's hand.

"We're glad you two could join us for dinner." Jordan immediately turned his attention to Annie. "And it is certainly good to see you, Annie."

Annie's expression changed from confident to cowering. Her forced smile made her look ill at ease. "Thank you."

Jordan motioned toward his right. "Let's go into the living room."

Ian followed Annie and his dad, hardly believing the change in Annie's demeanor. He hoped the evening wouldn't prove to be a disaster. He wished he could make Annie feel at home. He wanted to see a genuine smile rather than the one pinching her pretty features. Jordan pointed to the sofa covered in a brown-and-tan tweed fabric as he stood beside a brown armchair. Before Annie and Ian could maneuver around the dark wooden coffee table, Ian's mother, Doreen, appeared with a tray of appetizers.

Doreen put the tray on the coffee table, rushed over to Annie and gave her a hug. Stepping back, Doreen gazed at Annie. "You look wonderful. It does my heart good to see you."

"Thank you." Annie nodded, her smile still tentative. "It's nice to see you again, too."

"Please have a seat." Doreen sat on the chair next to Jordan's.

Ian stared at the couch—the only place left for Annie and him to sit. Had his parents conspired to make sure he and Annie sat together? As he took a seat at one end of the couch and Annie went to the other end, he decided it was probably better than sitting face-to-face.

His mom urged them to partake of the appetizers, and Jordan filled their glasses with some of his famous homemade peach iced tea. As Ian took a gulp of the tea to alleviate his parched mouth, he remembered how he and Annie would take glasses of this tea and sneak into the backyard and spike it with vodka, their parents never the wiser. He pushed the memory away. He didn't want to think about those times, but Annie's presence always seem to trigger those thoughts.

For a few minutes his parents talked about the beautiful spring weather and his mother's attempt at growing a vegetable garden this year. These non-threatening discussions were probably meant to put Annie at ease, but the stiff set of her shoulders told him that even these innocuous subjects made her feel uncomfortable.

A buzzer sounded in the distance, and Doreen hopped up from her chair. "Got to tend to the food."

Annie stood. "Do you need help?"

With a wave of her hand, Doreen glanced at Annie. "Oh, no, dear. You just sit back and enjoy. I've got everything under control. We'll eat in a few minutes."

"Okay." Annie returned to her seat, her uptight demeanor unchanged. Didn't his mom realize Annie wanted to escape to the kitchen? Apparently not. So Annie sat there, still as uneasy as the minute she'd walked in the door. There wasn't a thing he could do to help her.

Jordan scooted forward and gazed at Annie. "Did Ian mention that he's going to talk to the church board about more funding for The Village?"

Annie's eyebrows knit as her gaze flitted between the two men. "No."

Her one-word response hung in the air like an unanswered question. Ian wanted to stop the conversation right there. He feared where his dad was going with his inquiry. "I didn't have any reason to tell her."

Ian wanted to snatch back his response. That statement hadn't come out right. It sounded as if her opinion didn't matter. This evening was going from bad to worse. He wished his mom had asked Annie to help, then he wouldn't be dealing with this.

"She should know, since she's going to help you with the finances." Jordan nodded at Annie. "And

I think it would be good if you talked to the congregation about how The Village is helping you."

Annie's eyes widened and her mouth hung open as she looked from Jordan to Ian. "I don't know."

"Well, think about it. Ian can give you some pointers."

Before Annie could respond, Doreen appeared in the doorway. "Food is ready. So come and eat."

Ian quickly joined his mother. "I'm ready."

"Good." Doreen linked her arm through his, then glanced over her shoulder at Annie and his dad, who followed close behind. "I fixed one of Annie's favorites."

"You did?" Annie drew closer.

"You're our special guest, so I thought I should make something especially for you. I remembered how much you liked my spaghetti pie."

"Yum. I do, and I haven't had it in years. This is a real treat. Thanks."

"You're more than welcome." Doreen led the way into the kitchen. "I thought we'd eat here in the nook. It's cozier than the dining room."

The thought of cozy didn't help Ian's appetite; nor did his dad's invitation for Annie to speak to his congregation about her experience at The Village. She hadn't been there that long. Would he be expected to accompany her? What did she think about it? The questions poured through his mind as his dad said a prayer of thanksgiving for the meal.

When the prayer ended, everyone helped themselves to the food. Silence filled the room for several minutes as they ate. Ian kept hoping Annie wouldn't bring up their interrupted conversation. He got his wish as the talk turned to Annie's children and her upcoming court appearance. She produced a ragged photo of her and the kids taken at the rehab center several weeks before her release.

"Oh, they're so cute." Doreen gushed over the kids as if they were her own grandchildren.

"Thanks. I can hardly wait to be with them again, and this time I'm going to be the mother they can count on—the mother I should have been all along."

"And I pray you'll succeed." Doreen reached over and patted Annie's arm. "My grandkids live too far away, and they're growing up so fast. That reminds me. I have toys my grandkids have outgrown. After dinner we can look at them, and you can have whatever you want for Kara and Spencer. I've been meaning to give them to the church nursery, but this is a better idea."

Annie's eyes grew wide. "Thanks so much."

Ian didn't say anything, but he hoped his mom wasn't building up Annie's hopes. The court might decide against reuniting her with her children.

"Ian, are you listening?" His mother's voice shook him from his thoughts.

Ian grimaced. "Sorry. What did you say?"

"Do you have room in your car for the toys?" Doreen gave him a pointed look.

"I've got plenty of room." Ian wished his mom wasn't so pushy. Annie had never pushed him. She'd let him make his own decisions. That's one of the reasons he'd liked her from the start. He tamped down that thought. He didn't need to be thinking good things about Annie, but he shouldn't be thinking bad things, either. His mind was a mess. Annie was turning his world upside down again. He couldn't let that happen.

For the rest of the meal, Ian listened to Annie and his parents discuss a wide variety of topics. He'd forgotten how smart she was. She seemed more like her old self. At least that's what Ian tried to tell himself. But who was the real Annie? Had he ever really known her? Trying to find out now would only bring him trouble.

He'd moved on, hadn't he?

On Monday Annie jogged across the quad on her way to the finance meeting. The air smelled of sunshine and the earthy odor of spring. She'd prepared all weekend for this meeting. Would they be impressed with her recommendations, or would they dismiss what she had to say? She had to have a positive attitude.

Annie hadn't seen or talked to Melody or Ian

since the dinner at the Montgomery home. The visit had gone surprisingly well, even though she'd sensed Ian's unease about the whole thing. Even helping her with the toys for the kids had caused him discomfort. He obviously hadn't wanted to be alone with her in her apartment. He'd also managed to avoid her again at church on Sunday. She had to face reality. He didn't like being with her.

Annie had spent the preceding days in the library searching for more job opportunities. She'd sent her résumé to four more places early this morning. She couldn't go on avoiding the inevitable. Today she would have to tell Melody about not getting the first job. Could she find a job before her court date in three weeks? Scott didn't think it would matter since she was actively trying to find one, but Annie wanted every possible thing to be in her favor.

Despite having to deal with Ian again, she was looking forward to this meeting. She needed things to do besides search for a new job and keep her apartment in order. At least the appointment would provide something temporary to occupy her time. She would have to look for more volunteer activities at The Village. She wanted to stay busy—less chance to think about her old life. She had to think about the future and not the past.

When Annie walked into the designated library conference room, Melody was the lone occupant.

Maybe this was the best time to give her the news about the job. "Hi, Melody."

"How was your dinner meeting with Ian's parents?"

"It was fine. Doreen gave me toys for Kara and Spencer." Annie paused, wondering how much she should say. Melody seemed like a safe confidante, but Annie's experience with real girlfriends was limited. Growing up, she'd kept pretty much to herself. She'd been a loner when she was a kid. Now she couldn't image closing herself off from others.

"Super. The kids will love the toys. Not much longer till your hearing."

"I know, and there's something I need to tell you before the others get here."

Melody wrinkled her brow. "What's that?"

"I didn't get that job." Annie hung her head, afraid to see Melody's reaction.

"I'm sorry to hear that, but you'll find something else."

Annie grimaced. "I don't know. I'm not sure anyone will hire me because of my past."

"That's not true. We work with companies who are willing to hire people in recovery."

"Oh, so that's why I got the interview so quickly."

"Only partly. You have a great résumé."

"Then why didn't I get the job?"

"What did they say when they called?"

Annie shrugged. "That they hired someone else.

I've known for several days, but I was afraid to tell anyone."

"There's no reason not to tell us. We're here to help. Besides, you have to remember that several other people interviewed for that job. Only one person got it."

"Okay. I sent out four résumés this morning." Annie frowned. "But I suppose I didn't send them to the wrong places."

"Wherever you sent them will be fine." Melody nodded. "I want to assure you that there are companies out there who work with people from The Village."

Annie didn't know how to react. She wanted to be grateful for whatever opportunities The Village offered, but she hoped she didn't get a job for the wrong reasons. "Thanks."

"If you want more practice with interviews, just let me know." Melody's phone buzzed as it lay on the table. She answered it, a frown knitting her brow. "Sure, okay. We'll be waiting."

"Problems?"

"Yeah. Adam had car trouble, and he called Ian to get him. They got stuck in traffic. So they're going to be late." Melody shook her head.

Annie leaned forward. "Since Ian isn't handling my case, please don't tell him that I didn't get the job."

Melody raised her eyebrows. "Should I ask why you're worried about what Ian thinks?"

Annie wished she could take back her request. Now she had to do more explaining, and she didn't have a clear explanation herself. "From our recent conversations I've gathered that he doesn't have much confidence that I can succeed."

"Did he actually say that?"

Annie tried to think back over their conversations. Had he actually said those words? "No. He just doesn't trust me."

"Why is that?"

"He didn't tell you?"

Melody shook her head. "So why doesn't he trust you?"

Annie wished the others would show up so she didn't have to answer Melody's question. Annie had opened her mouth, and now she had to face a predicament of her own making. "I don't know whether you noticed, but he wasn't exactly thrilled when we talked about having me on the finance committee."

"Yeah, I noticed from the first time I mentioned it."

"He has good reason not to trust me."

"And why is that?" Melody asked.

Annie hoped this was the last bad chapter in her life that she would have to reveal. "After our divorce, my life continued to spiral downhill. I moved in with this guy who kept me supplied with booze and drugs. We had two kids. A few years ago, I was in bad shape after losing my job, and I needed money. My low-life boyfriend had split because kids cramped his style. So I went to see Ian. He gave me money because he couldn't stand to see my kids suffer, but I didn't use it for the kids. I used it to buy more drugs. I also stole his ATM card and helped myself to some of his money." Gripping the arms of his chair, Annie waited for Melody's reaction.

"Wow! Did he press charges?"

Annie sighed. "No, but he tracked me down and confronted me about it. We had a terrible argument. That was the last time I ever saw him until I came here."

Melody patted Annie's arm. "Thanks for sharing this with me. I know you didn't have to. Now I understand Ian's reluctance to include you in the finances."

"I figured it was better this way. The more you know the more you can help me."

"I'm glad you feel comfortable enough with me to share more of your story."

"Thanks for being my friend."

"I'm glad you think of me as a friend." Melody smiled. "Would you be interested in joining with the other women in your building for Bible study? I didn't ask you at first because you aren't dealing with abuse issues as they are, but I think we can all learn together no matter what our issues."

"I'd love to. Thanks for inviting me."

"Glad to have you." Melody glanced at her phone. "Adam and Ian should be here soon. I'm kind of happy they were late since we've had this chance to talk."

As Annie nodded, Ian and Adam rushed into the room.

"Sorry we're late, but that old car of mine is giving me fits again." Adam settled into his chair. "Let's get this meeting underway. I'd like to open with a prayer."

Everyone nodded as Adam bowed his head. While he prayed, Annie thanked God for the talk she'd had with Melody and joined in Adam's request for solutions to their financial problems. When Adam finished praying, he welcomed Annie to the committee and greeted Melody. He gave each of them a packet of papers.

Annie cast a surreptitious glance at Ian as she leafed through it. She wondered how he felt today about her being part of this committee. Had anything changed since Melody had first suggested Annie be a part of this? He was busy looking at his packet, and he'd given her nothing more than a nod when he and Adam had come into the room. Maybe it was the speed of their entrance that seemed to have him preoccupied. She tried to dispose of her negative thoughts and focused her attention on the financial report.

Adam eyed Annie. "Since you're the new voice on this committee, I'd like to hear from you first."

"Certainly." Annie's heart pounded as she opened her notes. "Thanks for asking for my input."

"What advice can you give us?" Ian's question came across as a challenge.

Annie gathered her thoughts. She wanted to help The Village, and she wanted to impress Ian. Was she hoping for too much? "I don't know that I'm going to be giving you any advice—more like observations. Then we can do a little brainstorming."

"I like that approach." Melody gave her a smile.

Annie smiled and cleared her throat. "I see from the report that you have cut your budget substantially and you don't have many other places to cut."

"So we're stuck? Nothing we can do but let the board shut us down? Is that what you're saying?" Ian stood. "I'm not going to let that happen even if I have to forfeit my salary."

Taken aback by Ian's outburst, Annie leaned back in her chair. She wasn't sure whether to continue or give Ian the floor.

Adam nodded at Annie. "Go ahead, Annie. Ian can have his say later."

Returning to his seat, Ian didn't look Annie's way. "I didn't mean to interrupt."

"I'm sure you won't have to forfeit your salary."

Annie shuffled through her papers. "I didn't say there was no place to cut, so I'm sure we can find more if we all work together. The one place where we can save money is with these vendor contracts. We can renegotiate many of these or find new vendors with cheaper prices."

"Will we get inferior products with cheaper prices?" Melody tapped a pen on the table. "I don't think we have to have top-of-the-line, but we shouldn't settle for poor quality."

Annie nodded. "I agree, but I'm certain we can get better prices."

"Is that your solution? Will that save us enough money?" Ian's disagreeable input hadn't diminished.

Trying to remain calm, Annie shook her head. She obviously wasn't making much of an impression on Ian. "Newly negotiated contracts will save us money, but that isn't the entire solution."

"What more do you have?" Adam asked.

"I have several other ways you can save money. Some are small, but the little things can add up." Annie waited for a moment, expecting Ian to object. When he didn't she continued. "I noticed that you send out a quarterly newsletter, which is good, but we need to send the majority of those letters as email. It'll save a lot on postage."

"How do you propose we do that when we don't have email addresses?" Ian asked.

Annie forced herself not to react to Ian's hostility. "I'm not sure, but I thought that's one of the things we can brainstorm."

"That sounds good." Melody shot Ian a perturbed look.

Annie smiled to herself. So Ian was getting on Melody's nerves, too. He wasn't thrilled about her presence here, but she couldn't figure out his sour attitude. It wasn't like him. He liked to speak his mind, but he usually did so in a diplomatic way. Something wasn't right with him, but she couldn't let that detour her from her plan. "I also noticed you have a lot of churches who support The Village. When was the last time anyone went to visit these churches?"

The room was silent for a moment. Finally, Adam leaned forward, his hands steepled as he put his elbows on the table. "That's a good question, and I don't have the answer." He glanced around the table. "Anyone else?"

Both Ian and Melody shook their heads.

Annie half raised a hand. "If it's been over a year, you should make an effort to line up a missions moment in each church. There are always new members who may not know about this ministry, and they may be willing to be a child's sponsor or donate in some other way. I have some ideas about that."

"Excellent." Adam nodded. "Give us your ideas."

Annie glanced toward the window. "Every time I cross the quad, I see the fountain. It's lovely, but it costs money to keep it running."

"Are you suggesting we shut it off?" Ian crossed his arms over his chest as he leaned back in his chair.

Annie shook her head. "We should definitely keep it running. I was thinking about getting people to sponsor the fountain for special occasions—like birthdays, anniversaries, holidays or some other event. If you want to do something like that, you could put it in the next newsletter that goes out. Also I think we should promote the campus store— for donations. Is there any way you could locate the store off campus where the public could shop? You could earn money from the sales."

"I like that idea as long as we have an off campus location. We keep security tight here because of the abused women we house, so we can't have the general public coming to the campus." Melody smiled.

"I'd be glad to check into off-campus sites." Annie smiled back, glad at least someone liked her idea. "That's all I have."

"But won't an off-campus site cost money in rent?" Ian eyed her.

"Not if we could find a church who would donate a room or even someone who owns a storefront they're not using and would be willing to donate its use for us. It never hurts to ask." Annie held her breath as she waited for a response.

"It's definitely something we can look into." Adam nodded. "Thanks, Annie, for volunteering to check for us. Also, you've presented us with some good ideas."

"Thanks." Annie smiled bigger, her heart lighter even though Ian didn't seem to share Adam's assessment.

"Unless someone else has something to add, I think this is where we need to do that brainstorming." Adam flipped the page on the legal pad where he'd been taking notes.

Melody nodded and Ian even mumbled his agreement. Annie gave a mental sigh of relief. She'd made a successful presentation even if Ian hadn't voiced an enthusiastic approval.

For the next hour the group went through the budget line by line and found more items to cut. They made plans to implement Annie's suggestions. Adam jokingly congratulated Annie for bringing them into the twenty-first century. By the time they finished, Annie had a renewed confidence. After they agreed to meet again in a week, Adam closed the meeting with prayer. Following the prayer, Annie gathered her things and headed for the door.

As she stepped into the hallway, Adam caught up

to her. "I want to thank you again for your valuable input. You're a real asset to the team."

"Thank you. I'm glad to contribute." Annie only wished Ian felt the same.

Adam stopped when they reached the door. "I was very impressed with your work on the finances, and I'd like to offer you a temporary job. The pay won't be much, but the work is something you could use on your résumé while you search for full-time work."

"What kind of temporary job?"

"You'd continue to work with Ian and Melody on the finances, helping to implement the changes we talked about today."

Grimacing, Annie didn't know for sure what to say. "I appreciate the offer. I don't want to sound ungrateful, but if you're trying to find ways to cut, how can you pay me?"

"That's a good question." Adam smiled. "I think the suggestions you made today will more than make up for the little bit we're going to pay you."

Annie smiled in return. "Thanks so much. I'll work really hard to earn that money."

"I know you will." Adam nodded. "Your first assignment will be to contact churches to set up presentations. I'll get you the list."

"Jordan Montgomery has already asked me to talk to his congregation. At first, the thought of talking to them petrified me, but I want to do whatever it takes to help The Village."

"Excellent. That's a good start. And I'll also get you information so you can start working on the email addresses for the newsletter."

"I'm excited about this work. Thanks again." Annie pushed open the door as Adam headed back down the hallway.

Annie stood on the stoop just outside the door and let the sunshine warm her face. Even though she didn't get that first job, God was providing a different opportunity. She loved being productive. She should never have let her life become such a mess. As she hurried across the quad, she made a promise to quit looking back. She couldn't undo the past. Living for today was the important thing.

Chapter Six

Ian stood in the conference room and stared out the window. Annie was hurrying across the quad. She stopped in front of the fountain. Was she thinking about her sponsorship idea? Why had he challenged every suggestion she made? Probably because she made him crazy. Her pixie good looks and brilliant mind were things he didn't want to think about.

His behavior at the meeting had been uncalled-for even if she did set off his conflicting feelings. She was here, and she wasn't going away anytime soon. He would have to interact with her more often than he wanted. Getting a handle on his emotions was imperative, but he wasn't sure how to do that. He'd been struggling with this ever since she had arrived, and he hadn't made any progress. It was time to change that.

While he watched her, she glanced down at her side. She reached into her pants pocket and pulled out her phone and answered it. She appeared to be having an animated conversation. She ended the call, shoved the phone back into her pocket and sprinted across the quad toward her apartment building.

As Ian contemplated Annie's actions, Adam entered the room. He set several papers on the table. "A copy of my notes from the meeting. I'll email you a portion of the donor list so you can start making calls."

"Thanks. I'll get started as soon as I can."

"One more thing." Adam gave Ian a pointed look. "I don't usually butt into other people's personal lives, but I want to know what's troubling you. You're not acting like yourself."

Ian was sure Adam knew Annie was the trouble, but he was letting Ian state the obvious, owning up to his problem. "I apologize for my negative attitude during the meeting."

Adam continued to give him that sharp stare. "And to what can we attribute your attitude?"

"I think you know. It's Annie."

"What are you going to do about her?"

Ian wondered whether he should tell Adam about the money incident with Annie. The old event still troubled him. He was torn between not denigrating Annie and defending his behavior. "I'll deal with it."

"I hope you do a better job going forward than you did today."

Ian nodded. "I will."

"A first step is to apologize to her. She did a good job, and she needs to know that you think so, too." Adam cleared his throat. "And I wanted you to know I offered Annie a temporary job working with the finances. So you'll be working together. I assume that isn't going to be a problem."

"It won't be." Ian hoped his expression didn't reveal his shock. He had to readjust his attitude. Adam was right. The whole apology thing wasn't going to be easy, but it was a first step in letting go of the past. It was something he thought he'd done but obviously hadn't. "I'll take care of that apology right now."

"Thanks." Adam clapped Ian on the back. "I know this is a difficult situation for you, but we need to work as a team to get things back on track financially."

Ian grabbed Adam's notes and followed him into the hallway. As Ian folded the papers and put them into his pocket, they went in opposite directions. Walking across the quad, Ian rehearsed what he was going to say to Annie. He let each version of his apology run through his mind. None of them seemed adequate. When he reached her apartment building, he opened the door just as Annie ran out, nearly bowling him over as she raced toward the door, her attention focused on her phone.

"Whoa." His pulse accelerated as he grabbed her shoulders. "You really ought to pay attention to where you're going. Why such a hurry?"

She stared up at him with those big blue eyes. His heart hammered. He could tell she was debating about her answer. "I need to see Melody. She's not answering her phone."

Ian looked Annie over from head to toe. She looked too good in her navy-blue business suit. She'd changed since their meeting. Why? "Melody had an appointment off campus after our meeting. Where are you going?"

Again she hesitated before answering. "I need a ride to see about a job. Melody said she'd give me a ride whenever I have a job interview."

"Was this something you had scheduled?"

"No. This just came up. They want me to come in today. I said sure because I thought Melody was here. I had no idea she'd left right after the meeting." Annie pressed her lips together. "Guess I should've checked first. I was so excited about the call that I didn't think first."

Ian counted to ten before he said anything. He didn't want to come across the way he had earlier today. At this point he shouldn't give advice. "I'll give you a ride."

"You will?"

"Of course. Where do you have to go?" Her question said a lot about where she thought they stood with each other. She didn't believe she could count on him for anything. Did he want that to change? Hadn't he determined only minutes ago that he was going to figure it out—the sooner the better?

"To that business park a few miles up the highway."

Ian nodded. "I know which one you mean—the one next to the big-box store."

"Yeah, that's the one."

"When do you have to be there?"

Annie glanced at her phone. "Not until one-thirty."

"Then you have over an hour before you even have to leave campus. You have plenty of time."

Annie looked worried. "I was hoping Melody could give me some last-minute pointers before I go in to talk to them."

"Annie, you'll do fine. Be yourself. You have the skills. You showed that this morning during our meeting." Ian wondered whether that statement alone would suffice as an apology. Probably not, but it was a good start. "Let's grab a quick bite to eat over at the senior center."

Annie grimaced. "I think I'm too nervous to eat."

Ian motioned toward the center. "I think a good visit with Cora and her gang is what you need."

Annie sighed. "I suppose."

Ian caught himself before he put a hand at her back to propel her in the right direction. The last thing he needed to do was touch her. He remembered his reaction when they'd bumped into each other at her apartment building. He didn't need any more of that kind of contact.

They walked in silence as Ian tried to sort through his feelings. They were a jumbled mess. This was his chance to apologize and put the rest of the day in a better perspective. Why couldn't he get the words to come out?

"So you think I should just be myself? What do you mean by that?"

Annie was thinking about his advice. He had to come through with something worthwhile. He wanted to be more of a hero than a heel. "You know...like you were this morning."

Annie stopped and stared at him. "You didn't think much of my presentation this morning. You questioned every suggestion I made."

The apology sat in his mouth like a wad of cotton. He was going to choke on it if he didn't spit it out. "And I'm sorry about that. I was wrong."

Annie stood there with her mouth open. She blinked a couple of times. "You're sorry?"

"Yes, will you forgive me for being a jerk?"

Annie nodded. "Forgiveness goes both ways. I need a lot more forgiveness than you. Can you forgive me for walking out on you, for stealing from you, for involving you in a disastrous lifestyle?"

Wow! God was certainly working on him today. The forgiveness he needed to work on went way beyond the stolen money. It went to the core of the hurt—the one he'd never forgotten—the one he'd let fester in his heart and keep him from forgiving her. He'd been stuck in the past, and he hadn't even known it. Today could be a new start, but he had to be honest with himself and with her. "Annie, I…"

"I know it's a lot to ask." She started walking again, almost as if she didn't want to hear his response or at least look him in the eye while he struggled with it. "Adam offered me a temporary job after the meeting, so I'll start paying you back the money soon."

Ian nodded. "Yes, Adam told me. I'm happy for you."

"Thank you. I told Melody how I stole from you."

"You did?"

"Yeah, I needed to explain your reluctance to have me on the committee." Annie stopped again. She straightened her shoulders and looked him right in the eye. "Can we be friends?"

Ian shook his head. "I don't know what we can be. It's too complicated, and I have to admit I'm not over the hurt. I need to work on that forgiveness— not only forgiving you, but forgiving myself for not saying what we were doing was wrong."

"You did eventually."

"Yeah, but it was too late."

"You can't put that on yourself. I made my own decision." Annie tapped her chest. "We're each responsible for what we did."

"But I feel like I let you down."

"We let each other down, but in the end we have to answer for our own sins."

"Thank God for sending a savior."

Annie smiled. "Thank God for His mercy."

"That's something we can agree on. Let's go get something to eat before we run out of time. We have to get you to that interview."

"Believe me, I'll pass on lunch before I miss that interview."

After signing into the assisted-living facility, they quickly got their food. Like the last time they'd eaten here, Ian was in charge of getting the drinks. Annie immediately spotted Cora, Ruby and Liz and headed in their direction. The elderly ladies were all smiles as Annie and Ian joined them.

"You're just the people we needed to see." Cora tapped a finger on the table.

"And why is that?" Ian placed the drinks on the table.

"We want you two to join us in our weekly dominoes game this evening at six." Cora grinned and Ruby and Liz agreed. "Usually we draw a pretty good crowd. And since it's mostly us seniors, the game ends early."

Ian ate his meal and wondered whether he was imagining the conspiratorial looks that passed between the three ladies. Were they trying to push Annie and him together? Paranoia tripped through his mind. Not good.

"Oh, that sounds like fun!" Annie poked him in the arm. "Don't you think?"

It didn't sound like fun, but he wasn't going to say so. He'd never enjoyed playing board games, even when he was a kid. "I'll reserve judgment."

"So then you're in, right?" Eyeing him, Ruby grinned. "We have a great time."

"I guess you've convinced me that this is something not to miss." Ian continued to eat, hoping the conversation would take another turn.

It did as the ladies started asking Annie about her job interview. In between bites, Annie explained how she had applied for a lot of jobs online. While the women chatted, Ian stewed. Everything about today had changed his relationship with Annie. Forgiveness topped the list of changes he promised to make in his life.

The only problem with forgiving Annie and putting the past behind him was the unresolved feelings for her that surfaced whenever they were together. How was he going to deal with his feelings without the buffer of his unforgiving attitude and hurt? Take those away, and he was vulnerable to so many things about her.

He had to keep his distance, but that wasn't going to happen when they had to work together on the finances and visit churches together. And now he'd been coerced into playing dominoes with Annie and a bunch of senior citizens. He needed a suit of armor to ward off her charm. All those things that had attracted him to her when they were teenagers still called to him. He'd traded unforgiveness for the chance to let her break his heart again. He had to do everything in his power not to let that happen.

After the interview, Annie sat on a bench near the office building waiting for Ian to pick her up. When he'd volunteered to give her a ride, his offer confirmed to Annie that he was genuinely excited about this opportunity for her. He'd told her from the beginning that he wanted her to succeed, but beyond that he couldn't say whether they could even be friends. The thought saddened her. But it was probably for the best. Friendship with Ian could entice her to want more—more than was wise for either one of them.

She felt equally wary about the interview she'd just had. The meeting with the group who was hiring had gone only okay. For two hours Annie talked with them as they bombarded her with questions. Strangely enough she was thankful for the way Ian had challenged her at the finance meeting. Without realizing it, he'd prepared her for the tough grilling she had encountered at the job interview. But despite being able to hold her own, she didn't have a good feeling about this job prospect.

Just as she told herself not to let negative thoughts flood her mind, Ian arrived. He looked over at her as she got into the car. "Did the interview go badly?"

Annie shrugged. "Not badly, but I didn't get the feeling that I'll get a call back. You know how you can sense those things."

"You never know. You could be wrong, and even if you're not, it was good practice." Ian started the car and pulled out onto the road.

"You're trying to put a positive spin on this."

"Why not? You have the temporary job for now, and you just keep looking."

Annie sighed. "I know. It's just that sometimes it all seems so impossible."

"Remember. Everything is possible with God. He knows the perfect job for you."

Ian seemed so sure of God and of himself. Since he'd been sober, had he ever thought about drinking or doing drugs? Did he ever have doubts? Annie wanted to ask, but she pressed her lips together to keep the question from popping out. They rode in silence the rest of the way.

When he pulled his car to a stop in the parking

lot near her apartment, she thought about that question again. She didn't know what answer the question would bring, but she was going to ask it. "Do you ever feel like getting high or having a drink like we used to?"

Ian stared at her as if he couldn't believe what he'd just heard. He leaned toward her as he put one arm over the steering wheel. "Why are you asking me this, Annie?"

"Because I want to know." Her heart hammering, she held her breath. Would he answer?

"I mean why are you asking me this now?" Frowning, he shook his head. "Are you thinking such thoughts because you can't find a job?"

"No, I never got high because I was depressed. I loved the euphoria. I loved to party." Annie grimaced. "So I wondered whether you ever—"

"Whether I ever think about taking a drink?"

"Yeah. That."

"Are you?"

Annie wished she could undo this conversation. Why had she asked the question? The answer— She wanted someone who understood the temptation. Melody didn't know what it was like to crave the next drink or the next hit—to squander everything good for the chance to get high. But Ian did. Annie finally nodded her head. "When you came to pick me up, I had this fleeting thought about going out with you and getting a drink just for the fun of it. I don't know why."

A slight smile curved one side of Ian's mouth. "That was the difference between you and me. I used drinking to forget my troubles, but you liked to drink to have fun."

At least he didn't seem to think badly of her. "Maybe we aren't that different. After all, when I was high, I didn't have to think about how my parents didn't care about me. But you used to drink with me to have fun."

"That's because I liked being with you. I thought we were having fun together, but we were only kidding ourselves." His expression turned sober. "I don't want to return to that way of life."

"Neither do I, but I'm scared that I can't be strong enough like you."

Ian shook his head. "I'm not that strong. I'm in a recovery group."

"Here on campus?"

Shaking his head, Ian gave her that wry smile again. "You know most people here don't know anything about my former addictions. I meet with a group at a church several miles from here. Has Melody connected you with one?"

"Not exactly. I'm doing a Bible study with the ladies who live in my apartment building."

"Good. At least that's a start. Remember. Take it one day at a time. Today I'm clean and sober."

Annie lowered her gaze as she twisted her hands in her lap. "I know that's the way it's supposed to be, but I worry about tomorrow and all the days to come."

"Annie, look at me."

She didn't want to look at him, because seeing him made her remember all she'd thrown away— all she wished she could recapture. But could they be good for each other ever again? Her head said no, but her heart said yes. Neither her head nor her heart had any control over what Ian thought about the situation. Finally, she forced herself to look at him. "What?"

"I want you to remember this verse from Matthew. 'Therefore do not worry about tomorrow, for tomorrow will worry about itself. Each day has enough trouble of its own.'"

"Yeah, trouble. That's for sure."

"Don't think about the trouble. Think about the good things God has given you today."

"Okay."

After they got out of the car, Annie watched him walk away with questions crowding her mind. Was he looking forward to tonight and dominoes with the seniors, or was it only another obligation? He seemed friendly, but he had said earlier that he didn't know whether they could be friends. Dreaming about getting back together with Ian was futile no matter how much she wanted that to happen. She had to move on, but how was that possible when something was always bringing them together?

Laughter and boisterous voices bounced off the walls of the dining hall in the assisted-living facility. Ian chuckled as Annie raised her hands in triumph as the two of them won another game of dominoes. He had dreaded this evening and spending time with Annie because he was afraid it would trigger too many bad memories from the past. Instead, he was actually enjoying their time together.

Ian gave Annie a high five. "I picked the right partner for this game."

"Absolutely." She grinned at him. "I used to play this at the rehab center, so I've had a lot of practice."

"Do you think it's fair for you young people to be beating us old folks?" Cora chuckled.

Ian turned the dominoes to prepare for a new game. "Completely fair. After all, you're the ones who insisted we play."

Cora shook her head as she got up to move to another table. "Next week Ruby and I will be prepared for a rematch."

"We're ready for the challenge," Annie called after them.

Ian liked seeing Annie in a fun and happy place. At the same time, he worried that spending more time with her could rekindle those old feelings he'd been thinking about. Is that what he wanted? Was it wise? He shouldn't contemplate that now. Just have fun and enjoy seeing Annie being joyful. He'd never seen her this happy in a sober state. She'd often found her happiness in a bottle of rum. He was glad to see that had changed.

When the evening came to an end, Annie and Ian were dominoes champions of the week. Annie hoisted the cheesy trophy—a cluster of dominoes glued to a gold-colored cup—over her head and grinned. Ian stood beside her as he relished her elation. Seeing her smile lessened his anxiety over what to do with their relationship. While Annie basked in their triumph, Cora, Ruby and Liz—the Three Musketeers as Annie had dubbed them—came over to extend their congratulations.

"Since you're so good at dominoes, we're going to challenge you to a different game. We play bridge on Tuesday nights. What do you say?" Cora asked.

"That sounds like fun." Annie looked at Ian. "What do you think?"

"Me?" Ian shook his head. "I don't play bridge."

"You can learn. It's challenging—good for the mind." Cora gave him a pointed look. "Annie can teach you."

Ian surveyed the group of women. What had he gotten himself into? "I have a lot of responsibilities, and I can't spend my time playing games."

Cora shook a finger at Ian. "All work and no play makes you—"

"Makes me conscientious."

Cora chuckled. "Okay, but give it some thought. You might like the game."

"We'll see." Ian looked at Annie. "Ready to go? I'll walk you back to your apartment."

"No need for that." Annie headed for the door.

Wondering if she was trying to avoid him, Ian fell into step beside her. "This is a relatively safe place, but it's dark. I'd feel better walking you home. Besides, I have to go in that direction to get my car."

"Okay."

As they left the building, Ian asked himself why he wanted to do this. Was he concerned for her safety, or did he want to spend more time with her? Tonight had shown him a different side of Annie—one he'd never seen. "I didn't realize you were so competitive."

"I learned it from Grandma and Grandpa Payton, especially Grandma. She taught me to play a lot of games." Looking over at him, Annie smiled. "As soon as I was old enough, we played for hours."

"I remember how upset you were when your grandparents passed away." As soon as Ian spoke, he wished he could take it back. He didn't want to remind Annie of unhappy times.

"I was, but I remember how kind you were to

me when that happened. You made me feel special, and I needed that."

Ian smiled and wondered what she would say if she knew the reason behind his kindness. She might not take it in the way he had intended. He'd been thrilled when his actions gained him the attention of cute little Annie Payton, who had ignored him up until that point. She'd made him feel special, too. Why had they ruined it?

He needed to change the subject. "Do you really want to play bridge? I always thought it was a game for old people."

Annie gave him a disgusted look. "I can't believe you said that. Not very PC. I know how to play."

"You're the only person our age who plays bridge."

"You aren't acquainted with everyone our age."

"True." Ian chuckled. "You don't have to get defensive. I just didn't realize you knew the game. Something your grandmother taught you?"

"Yeah."

"See. I told you the game was for oldsters."

"Quit teasing." Annie gave him a playful thump on the arm. "I'm serious. I can teach you how to play."

"I'm serious, too. I don't have much time for games." His heart racing from her touch, Ian looked at her as the security light illuminated her pretty features. Her mesmerizing blue eyes looked up at him. He gulped as his heart zipped. His gaze fell to her lips, and for a moment he was tempted to kiss her. No. That would be the worst possible thing he could do—play a game he couldn't win. He had to get out of here. "Good night, Annie. Thanks for the victory."

She punched in the building code. "Good night. Bridge lessons are waiting anytime."

Without responding, Ian waved as he headed to his car. An evening spent with Annie had him thinking wrongheaded thoughts. He couldn't let those thoughts turn into actions…could he? He should take it just as he dealt with his sobriety—one day at a time.

Chapter Seven

The musical tones of Ian's cell phone made him sit straight up in bed. The first hints of daylight peeked around the edge of the blinds as he rubbed the sleep from his eyes. He picked up the phone. Six o'clock. Why was Scott Bartlett calling at this hour of the morning?

Today was Annie's custody hearing. She'd waited five weeks for this day since coming to The Village. Was Scott calling about that?

Ian tapped the screen on his phone to take the call. When he heard Scott's wife on the line, Ian suspected something was wrong. "Cindy, this is Ian. Why are you calling?"

"I've got bad news. I had to take Scott to the hospital. He's having an emergency appendectomy." Ian couldn't mistake the distress in Cindy's voice. "He said I should call because he's supposed to be in court this morning—a favor he was doing for you."

"Tell Scott not to worry. I'll take care of it." Ian wished that weren't the case, but he would have to do it. "I'll be praying for you both. Leave a message to let me know how he's doing."

"Thanks. Talk to you later."

Ian hopped out of bed. How would Annie take this turn of events?

After grabbing a breakfast bar and instant coffee, he headed to his office. He had to get the briefs Scott had shared with him. The case Scott had prepared looked solid. Ian couldn't see any reason the judge would refuse to reunite Annie with her children unless there was something Scott and he didn't know about. Ian gathered his things and put them into his briefcase and headed toward Annie's apartment to give her the news. Ian prayed she would accept his representation without a problem.

Since the evening they had played dominoes together three weeks ago, they'd only seen each other in passing. She'd never mentioned the bridge lessons again. He wasn't sure whether he was happy or sad about that. He'd been so busy with his cases and court dates that some days he felt he met himself coming and going. Lunch with his dad was a casualty, as well. Now this added to all the craziness.

There was no answer when he knocked on Annie's door. He knocked again. Still nothing. He pulled out his phone and dialed her number. The phone rang and rang until his call went to voice mail. He left a message, his stomach churning. What did he do now?

Ian went next door and knocked, hoping Annie's neighbor could give him information. But none of her neighbors seemed to be home, either. He leaned against the wall in the hallway and shook his head. Why was no one home? Finally, he called Melody, but she wasn't answering her phone, either.

What was going on? He felt he was in some kind of alternative universe where he couldn't communicate with the people on the other side. The best thing he could do was go to the courthouse. When the others showed up, they would be surprised to see him. While he drove, he prayed that everything would work out. As he pulled into the parking area near the courthouse, his cell phone rang. After maneuvering into a spot, he picked up the phone. "Melody, I've been trying to get a hold of someone."

Melody chuckled. "You sound a little frazzled."

"Is Annie with you?"

"Yes, we're only minutes away from the courthouse."

"That's a relief."

"Why are you saying that?"

Ian proceeded to explain what had happened with Scott. "So I'll be representing Annie today in the hearing. Will you let her know?"

"Sure."

"How come neither you nor Annie answered your phones?"

"The Bible study group I lead was having a prayer meeting with a group of seniors over at the assisted-living center. We were praying about Annie's hearing."

"Good to know." Why had he been left out of the loop? "I'll see you momentarily."

Ian sat in his car and contemplated his reaction. For a fleeting moment he'd thought something bad might have happened to Annie. After she'd walked out and stolen from him, he'd told himself he didn't care what happened to her. Now he had to face the fact that he cared—a lot. What did that mean for his peace of mind?

Getting out of the car, he shook the question away. He didn't need to let his feelings get mixed up in this case. This was about the law and whether Annie could satisfy the court that she could take care of her children. His involvement should start and stop there. As he approached the door to the courthouse with its giant clock tower looking down on him, his parents approached from the other direction.

"Mom, Dad." Ian waved a hand over his head. They stopped and turned in his direction. "What are ya'll doing here?"

"We could ask the same." His dad held the door open.

As they went inside, Ian explained the circumstance that had brought him to court. "You still haven't explained why you're here."

"We're here to support Annie." His mom gave him a sympathetic look. "I know the divorce and everything was very hard on you, but I still love Annie like a daughter, and I want things to go well for her."

Nodding, Ian swallowed hard. "I do, too."

While they talked in the cavernous hallway, Melody and Annie came through the door. There were greetings all around, and Ian could see that having his parents there meant a lot to Annie as her eyes welled up with tears. What would it be like if he and Annie got back together again? No. He couldn't let that kind of thinking fill his mind. It was crazy. This stuff with his parents was making him feel things he shouldn't feel at all. He was here as her lawyer. That was it.

In the next few minutes, Annie introduced everyone to Pastor John. He had come to testify on Annie's behalf. While Annie made the introductions, Ian went over his opening statement. He hoped he could do a good job on short notice.

Ian approached Annie and caught her attention. "Are you ready?"

"Yes." She nodded, her expression apprehensive. "Are *you* ready to represent me? This has been dumped in your lap at the last minute. Besides,

I've done a lot to hurt you, and this is just one more mess of mine you have to deal with."

"I've been keeping up with your case and have all of Scott's files. And honestly, I don't mind." Surprisingly, he meant it.

Annie nodded but her worry didn't seem to ease. "Since I haven't been able to get a regular job, do you think that'll count against me?" Annie pressed her lips together.

"You're looking. That's what counts and, besides, you have the temporary job at The Village. I believe you have a strong case, Annie."

"Thank you." She looked up at him and smiled.

Ian's pulse zipped. He couldn't let her smile distract him. "Let's go into the courtroom. The hearing will start in a few minutes. Everyone who is here to testify on your behalf will have to wait outside the courtroom until they're called."

Standing, Annie nodded. "Let's go."

As soon as they were seated, Ian focused his attention on his opening statement. When Annie had first come to The Village, he hadn't believed most of what he was about to tell the judge. There was no way he could have honestly represented Annie, but today he had a different perspective. He could see that she'd changed. She did want to put her life in order, and he wanted to help her.

When the middle-aged female judge entered the courtroom, everyone rose. The woman had an intimidating presence. Her short black hair matched her robe. Ian sensed Annie's trepidation as she stood beside him. The connection between them reminded him of the early days of their relationship. Did he want to revisit that time and those feelings? He didn't know, and this wasn't the time or place to try to figure it out. He focused his attention on what the judge was saying.

As Ian stood to give his opening statement, he said a silent prayer to God. He had to leave this whole process in His hands. God knew whether Annie deserved to have her children back.

After the judge had heard Ian and the folks who had come to testify on Annie's behalf, the attorney for DFCS swore in Annie's caseworker, Elena Lamb. He listened to the woman's testimony about Annie's numerous relapses. The Annie the caseworker was talking about was the old Annie. Why couldn't the woman see how Annie had changed? Getting to know her again had little by little changed his mind about her. He didn't understand why the caseworker wanted to keep Annie away from her children. But hadn't he had the same attitude when Annie first came to The Village?

When the testimony concluded, the judge banged her gavel and Ian and Annie rose as the judge looked down on them. Annie stared straight ahead, not moving a muscle.

The judge surveyed the courtroom before focusing her gaze on Annie. "After listening to the testimony, it is my judgment that Annie Payton should have custody of her children."

A murmur floated through the courtroom, and Annie looked up at him, a little smile curving her lips. When the judge banged her gavel again, Annie quickly focused her attention toward the front.

"Quiet until I'm finished." The judge looked toward the caseworker. "The children will be returned to their mother under a Protective Order." The judge let her gaze settle on Annie. "Ms. Payton, you must continue to have clean drug screens, continue to look for employment and return to court every three months for a review."

The judge turned to the caseworker again. "You will arrange for a transitional meeting between Ms. Payton, her children and the foster parents within the next seventy-two hours. We want to make this transition as easy as possible and in the best interest of these children."

After the judge adjourned the proceedings and left the courtroom, Annie turned to Ian and threw her arms around him. "Thank you. Thank you. I can't thank you enough."

Hardly allowing himself to breathe, Ian put his arms around Annie and gently held her as she cried with happiness, her shoulders shaking as the tears flowed. Holding Annie reminded Ian of the time when their relationship was new and sweet and innocent. But it couldn't ever be that way again. Too much bad stuff had passed between them.

"I'm happy for you, Annie. You've worked hard to get Kara and Spencer back. You deserve this." Extricating himself from the embrace, he tried to push thoughts of Annie and him far, far away.

As he held Annie at arm's length, his parents joined them. He stood back as his dad and then his mom smothered Annie with hugs and congratulations. He was thankful for their presence and how it had rescued him from his troubled thoughts. He couldn't be part of Annie's life again. Why did he have to keep telling himself that?

Melody, Pastor John and other folks from The Village joined in the celebration with handshakes, hugs and laughter. As Ian took in the joy surrounding the group, Elena Lamb approached from the other side of the courtroom. He met her in the space in front of the judge's bench.

She smiled and held out her hand. "Congratulations. You've succeeded in reuniting your client with her children. I hope this will be a good thing for all concerned."

Ian shook the woman's hand, but he didn't believe she was happy about the outcome of this hearing. He wanted to ask why, but he wouldn't open up that subject. He only wanted to set up the time for the transitional meeting. When that was accomplished he ended the conversation.

Ian's dad came over and clapped him on the back. "Good job, son. We've invited everyone over to our house for a little lunchtime celebration."

"Okay. I'm glad she can celebrate with everyone." Ian glanced in Annie's direction.

Ian couldn't remember the last time he'd seen her so happy, even happier than when she'd won at dominoes. He liked the new Annie, and he couldn't help wondering how she felt about him. Was he crazy to consider rekindling his relationship with her? She'd broken his trust. He didn't know whether it could be repaired. Even with that thought lingering in his mind, he wasn't doing a very good job convincing himself that a new start with Annie would be a completely bad thing.

When Annie arrived at Jordan and Doreen's home, they greeted her with open arms and open hearts. She never realized how much Ian's parents had loved her. Her heart ached because she'd caused them pain as well as Ian. During their conversation at the courthouse, they'd reassured her that the past was forgotten. Jordan reminded her that God forgives and that as Christians they had to follow His example and forgive.

Their forgiveness made her heart lighter, but Ian still withheld his. At least he said he was working on it. She shouldn't be thinking about Ian. He wasn't even here to celebrate, but at least he'd been there for her today in court. Why was forgetting him so hard?

While Annie helped herself to the substantial spread on Doreen's dining room table, Ian walked through the front door. Her heart tripped. She was never going to get over him. She watched as his mom greeted him and led him into the dining room.

"Annie, look who's here." Doreen grabbed Annie's hand and pulled her closer.

"Hi, Ian." Annie's smile wavered as Ian looked at her. She should never have hugged him in the courtroom. What a mistake. Somehow she would have to find the time to apologize.

Ian looked at his mother, then over at Annie, as he shook his head and gestured toward Doreen. "You'd think the way she's acting we hadn't just seen each other in court."

"I wanted her to know you were here. I see how you men will huddle in a corner and never bother with us women." Doreen handed him a plate. "Help yourself."

Ian took the plate and put several items on it. "Mom, since you had this planned, you must've had a lot of confidence that Annie would win her appeal."

"Why not? We've been praying for weeks that Annie would be reunited with Kara and Spencer. You know what the scripture says in the gospel of Mark. 'Therefore I tell you, whatever you ask for in prayer, believe that you have received it, and it will be yours.'"

Ian nodded, acknowledging the truth of what his mother had said. "Thanks for the reminder."

Doreen patted his arm. "And besides, my handsome son is an excellent lawyer."

"You don't have to brag on me, Mom. I didn't prepare the case."

"Yes, but you knew who to ask when you couldn't, and in the end, you presented the case."

Annie tried to slip away while Doreen and Ian talked, but Doreen thwarted Annie's effort. "Annie, I'm sure you and Ian have things to talk about, so I'll leave you two alone."

Ian stared at Annie, a smile curving his mouth. "Do we have something to talk about?"

Annie nodded. This was the time to apologize. "I think so."

Ian gestured toward the back of the house. "Let's go out on the deck where we can have a little privacy."

"Okay." Annie followed him through the sliding-glass door onto the redwood deck overlooking the backyard. Tall pines shot toward the sun amongst the oaks and maples. Her heart beating in double time, Annie took a deep breath and wondered why they needed privacy.

Ian walked over to the railing and placed his plate on the top of it. He took a few bites of his food, then leaned on the railing with his forearms as he looked out at the yard and not at her. "What do you have to say?"

Should she bring up the hug, or leave it alone? Taking a long, slow breath, she joined him at the railing, but he continued to stare straight ahead. If she didn't apologize, she would still be second-guessing herself. With Ian she never knew which way to turn. She had to say something, or he'd get the crazy idea that she wanted to be alone with him. The idea wasn't so crazy. That was the trouble.

"Well?" Ian turned to look at her.

Her heart jumped into her throat, and she lowered her gaze to the deck. "I'm sorry I hugged you in the courtroom. It wasn't appropriate. I appreciate your help. That's all."

His footsteps sounded on the deck as he drew closer. "It's okay, Annie. You didn't do anything wrong."

She slowly raised her head. "You're sure?"

"Yes, I'm sure. Let's talk about Kara and Spencer."

Obviously, the hug meant nothing to Ian. He'd dismissed it without a second thought. "Sure. What did the caseworker say to you? I always got the feeling she didn't like me much and was never an advocate for reuniting me with my kids."

"Do you know why?"

Annie didn't want to explain, but she was sure

Ian already knew the answer. "You've said it yourself. You don't trust me to stay clean and sober, and neither does the caseworker. You've seen me relapse more than once, and so has she. I'm pretty sure that's why you didn't want to represent me in the first place."

Ian stepped even closer and took her by the shoulders. "You're right, but I see that you've changed. I believe in you."

"Thank you." That one statement had Annie wanting to fall into Ian's arms and stay there forever, but he wasn't ready for that, or was he? She stared up at him. For one instant she thought he was going to kiss her.

He dropped his hands and stepped away. "We'd better go inside and mingle."

"Sure." Had she imagined the almost kiss? Was it wishful thinking? *Think about your kids, not Ian.*

"There you two are." Melody hurried toward them. "I've got to leave for a meeting with a new resident. Ian, you can give Annie a ride home, can't you?"

"Yeah," Ian said as he grabbed his plate and finished the last bite of food.

"Great." Melody gave Annie a hug. "And congratulations again. I'm so happy for you."

"Thanks."

"Let me know if you need anything." Melody waved as she raced away.

Ian chuckled. "I don't think she slows down for a minute."

"She knows how to get things done." Annie digested Ian's comment and wondered how he felt about Melody. The senior ladies said there was no spark between Ian and Melody, but Annie wasn't convinced. While hints of jealousy roamed through her thoughts, all her feelings about Ian inundated her. Jealousy, worry, gratitude and the one that held the most sway—love. What was she going to do with that?

"I'm going to get some more food." Ian pointed to his empty plate.

"Go ahead. I'm good." Annie hoped for a few minutes alone to sort out her feelings.

"Ian. Oh, good. I found you." Doreen stopped him. "I have something to discuss with you and Annie."

Ian's expression portrayed annoyance. "And what would that be?"

"Mother's Day."

"Are you trying to give me hints for what you want?"

Doreen gave him a friendly swat. "No. I don't need gifts, just your time. Your father is taking me out to dinner, and I expect you to be there."

"Of course, I'll be there."

"And I want you to bring Annie and the children."

Annie didn't miss the panic in Ian's gray eyes,

but she would seem ungrateful if she tried to decline Doreen's invitation. Did Doreen realize she'd put Ian in a bad spot, or was she purposely trying to push them together?

"Don't you think you should ask Annie first? She's standing right here." Ian raised his eyebrows as he looked first at his mother, then at Annie.

"I want to make sure you would give her a ride to the restaurant since the two of you will be speaking during the services." Doreen put an arm around Annie's shoulders. "And I'll be sure to make arrangements for the children. I know it'll be a long morning for them and a strange environment."

"Mom, I think you're right. Don't you think it might be a bit much for them to handle, especially on top of the transition from foster care?"

Doreen waved a finger at Ian. "Yes, and that's why I thought it would be wonderful for you to bring Annie and the kids over for pizza on Saturday night. Then they'll have a chance to get to know us."

Again, Annie could see that Ian wasn't happy about his mother's planning. But she had Ian and Annie trapped. There was no way they could turn down the invitation. Annie forced a smile. "Thanks for thinking of us. I'm sure Kara and Spencer will enjoy the pizza. I was always good at ordering pizza."

"You were good about ordering anything." Ian gave her a smile.

"Please don't mention my lack of cooking skills." Annie tried to keep a straight face, but a smile persisted. "I had a mother who rarely cooked."

"I'd love to share some recipes with you." Doreen touched Annie's arm. "Would you like me to give you a few cooking lessons?"

"Mom, maybe Annie doesn't want cooking lessons."

Doreen looked quizzically at Ian. "Let Annie speak for herself."

"Yeah, like she's going to tell you she doesn't want your interference."

Annie stepped back as Ian and his mother argued—about her. Annie wanted to slink away, but before she could leave, Ian and Doreen both turned and stared at her. What could she say? Did she want to learn to cook? Yeah. For her kids. "I'd love some lessons."

"You would?" Ian's expression of disbelief nearly made Annie laugh.

"Yes." Annie glanced at Doreen. "Thanks for offering."

"My pleasure. I never had any girls to cook with, and I could never get my boys interested." Doreen clapped her hands together. "So this will be fun. We can make arrangements to get together some evening or on the weekend, whichever suits you. I can hardly wait."

Annie chuckled. "You might change your mind after you find out how helpless I am in the kitchen."

"I like a challenge." Doreen gave Annie a hug.

"Mom, since you two want to talk about cooking, do I have your permission to join the men?"

"Go." Doreen waved him out of the room, then turned to Annie. "I'm sorry if I seemed pushy."

"I don't mind. Oh, I didn't mean to imply you were pushy. I mean—"

"It's okay, Annie. I understand what you mean. Don't let Ian's talk change your mind."

Annie grimaced. "He knows I'm a terrible cook, so it doesn't surprise me that he thinks I wouldn't be interested in lessons."

"Sounds to me like my son has a lot of preconceived ideas about you."

"He knows me, or at least he knows the old me."

"Is he getting to know the new you?"

Annie thought about the times he'd reminded her of past mistakes. "I'm not sure."

Doreen looked over her shoulder as if she was checking to see who was there. Then she leaned closer. "I know Ian wouldn't want me to ask you this. And probably I shouldn't, but is there any chance you two might get back together again?"

Annie looked down at the golden oak plank flooring. It was almost as if Doreen knew the question Annie had been trying not to answer since she'd arrived at The Village. What could she say? She finally looked up and shook her head. "I don't see that happening. Too much bad stuff has gone on between us."

Doreen placed both hands over her heart. "I know this is wishful thinking on my part, but I would like to see it happen. I'm going to pray about it. You pray, too."

Annie shook her head. "We've hurt each other too much."

"That's true, but I still see this spark between you." Doreen nodded.

"But it takes more than a spark to repair a very damaged relationship." Annie wished she was brave enough to tell her former mother-in-law how much she still cared about Ian, but it would only flame Doreen's hopes. There was no sense in that, especially since Ian most likely didn't want anything to do with her. But what about that almost kiss on the deck? Her imagination? She couldn't rely on her own yearnings. She had to face reality. "I'm not sure we would be good for each other. We might bring each other down like we did before."

"But this time your relationship would have God at the center."

Annie wanted to put an end to this futile discussion, but she didn't know how to tell Doreen without hurting her feelings. "I don't mean to push your idea aside or say anything against Ian, but…"

"But you don't believe he cares about you."

"I didn't say that."

Doreen held up a hand. "I know you didn't, but I saw what happened between you two after Ian's accident. Yes, you were the one who walked out on him and filed for divorce, but I felt as though he walked out on you first. He spent his time studying with his law school study group. He didn't talk to you. It was as if he forgot you were there. I know you felt abandoned. I should've done more to help you through that time, but I thought you would think I was interfering. I stood silently by while I watched your relationship unravel. Now I wish I'd stepped in, even if I didn't know what I was doing."

How had Doreen known Annie's feelings so well? Could Doreen be the mother figure she'd been longing for? She wished she'd been a better daughter-in-law. "You shouldn't put any blame on yourself. I'm not sure either Ian or I would've taken your advice. Sometimes, I think the only thing we had in common was the booze and drugs."

"Do you still feel that way?"

"I don't know how I feel, and I don't know for sure what Ian thinks about me these days. I didn't mean to say bad things about him. I'm the one who chose a life of self-indulgence and debauchery over him. How can he forgive me for that? How can you?"

"We all need forgiveness."

Annie nodded. "I know that truth, but sometimes it's so hard to accept that I'm forgiven when I've hurt so many people."

Doreen patted Annie's arm. "Just know that you are, and Ian knows he's been forgiven, too."

"He has been nothing but helpful since I crashed back into his life again. And I appreciate your help, but talk about Ian and me getting back together isn't good." Annie wrinkled her brow. "Do you still want to teach me to cook?"

"Absolutely." Doreen sighed again. "I'm sorry I put you on the spot about Ian, but I couldn't help myself. I didn't want to stand silently by again if there was a chance that you could repair your relationship. You seem to be getting along so well, so I was kind of hoping. I'll be praying about it."

"Thanks." Annie hugged Doreen, then stepped away.

"Think about what I've said. God can work miracles."

Annie nodded but didn't say another word. She couldn't rely on false hope—hers or Doreen's.

Chapter Eight

Annoyed with the circumstance that had him spending more time with Annie than he'd bargained for, Ian put his car in gear and backed out of his parents' driveway. Time spent with Annie had him thinking about reconciliation. Was that wise?

He glanced over at her, sitting statuelike in the front passenger seat as he drove toward the main highway. "Did you enjoy your celebration?"

"Your parents were very gracious to host a party for me. You and your family have done so much for me. I can't thank you enough."

"They were glad to do it." Ian believed the sincerity of her statement, but he recognized her discomfort with the whole situation—the same discomfort he was feeling. Should he mention it or keep quiet? His mom had occupied a lot of Annie's time this afternoon. What did they discuss?

Cooking? Kids? Him? Was he being paranoid? He had to quit thinking about it.

"Despite what you think, I'm really glad your mom is going to teach me to cook. I want to fix good things for Kara and Spencer. I want to be a mother they can count on. They have a worthless father. They should have at least one good parent."

Annie's statement came out of nowhere, but he understood that she probably hadn't appreciated his comment about her lack of culinary skills. And her statement about the worthless father told him what he'd wanted to know about her relationship with her former boyfriend. She no longer had amorous feelings for another man. Maybe that wasn't such a good thing. The knowledge could have him contemplating another chance with Annie, but wasn't he already thinking that? "I didn't mean to make light of your interest in cooking. It just surprised me. I know you want to do what's best for your kids."

Looking over at him, she gave him a tentative smile, then turned away in silence. He had to concentrate on the road, not on her sweet little smile. She seemed so uncertain around him, not the vibrant young woman he'd seen talking with his parents. She would obviously rather be anywhere but with him. Her reaction to him ought to make it clear that she didn't have any thoughts of rekindling their relationship. So why did he?

While he took the entrance to the freeway, he thought about how he'd almost kissed her when they were on the deck together. Thankfully, his common sense had returned before he'd let the attraction take over his brain and tempt him to do something that would have been a disaster.

"I'm a little nervous about Kara and Spencer coming to live with me. They've only seen me a few times in the past year. Do you think they even know I'm their mother?"

Thankful for something to steer his thoughts in another direction, Ian shook his head. "I don't know what to tell you. Hopefully the transitional meeting will help with that. I'm sure there will be a period of adjustment, but everyone at The Village is there to help you and the kids adapt."

"You, too?"

Why was she asking him that? One minute she seemed to be pushing him away with her uneasiness and the next she was trying to involve him in her life. "If you want, but I'm not sure what help I can be. I don't know much about kids. Melody and the ladies in your Bible study group and even the senior ladies will be more help than I would be."

"But you'll be there if I need your help?"

Ian's pulse rocketed even as his heart melted. "I can try."

"Thank you."

That tender spot for Annie grew a little bigger.

He gripped the steering wheel tighter. Did he want to get that enmeshed in Annie's life? After all, he'd spent the past few years trying to forget her and the past few weeks trying to figure out how to deal with her presence at The Village. Could he help her and still maintain enough distance to keep himself from falling for her all over again? Was God changing his heart, or was he being a fool to honor her request?

So many questions. They'd haunted him over and over again since Annie's reappearance. As he neared their exit, he longed for another change of subject. "When we get back to campus, I think we should stop by the assisted-living facility and tell Cora and the group your news."

Annie smiled. "That's a fantastic idea."

Trying to tamp down his reaction to her praise, Ian parked near the assisted-living center. Annie popped out of the car as soon as he stopped. She headed to the center without waiting for him. He quickened his pace and joined her as she signed in. When they reached Cora's apartment, Ian knocked. They waited for a few moments. Then Ian turned to Annie. "Do you suppose she isn't in her apartment?"

"Is there someone we can ask?"

"I'll see if I can find one of the staff. Maybe they can tell us. Wait here in case she comes to the door."

Ian returned in a minute. "Cora's been moved to the nursing facility."

"Has something happened?"

"She's okay, but she had a fall late this morning and was taken to the hospital emergency room."

"Did she break something?"

Ian shrugged. "They didn't give me details. You know the privacy thing, but they released her to the nursing facilities here. They're keeping her there at least overnight just to be sure she's good to go back to her apartment. She can have visitors. Do you want to see her?"

"Absolutely." Annie didn't wait for him as she headed for the door.

When they reached Cora's room, the door was ajar and a nurse's aide had just delivered pitchers of ice-cold water to Cora and her roommate. Ian lightly rapped his knuckles on the door.

Sitting in the chair next to her bed, Cora looked their way. "Come in. Maybe you can talk these people into letting me go home. I'm fit as a fiddle. I took a little tumble this morning, and now they've got me in here."

Ian stood next to her chair and patted her shoulder. "You'll probably be out of here tomorrow."

"I'd better be. We've got dominoes tomorrow night, young man. You missed last week. Are you afraid I'll beat you this time?"

Ian saluted. "Yes, ma'am, I'll be there. I'm not afraid you can beat me."

"You'd better be there, or I'll come and get you." Cora waved her cane in Ian's direction, then looked at Annie. "Come here, sweet girl. I want to give you a congratulatory hug. Melody stopped by and told me your good news. Ruby and Liz were here, too. So they know. We're so excited to meet your children."

"Thank you." Annie stepped closer and gave Cora a hug. "Now you take care of yourself so you can go back to your apartment."

Cora waved a hand in the air. "Ever since I had that little stroke a year ago, they overreact to everything. But if I have to be somewhere other than home, I'd rather be here than in the hospital. The nurses here are super."

"Did I hear a compliment?"

Ian turned toward the door. Kirsten Bailey, one of the R.N.s at the extended-care facility, carried two small cups.

"You weren't supposed to hear that." Cora chuckled. "I need to keep you on your toes."

"Oh, you keep us on our toes." Kirsten handed Cora one of the little cups. "Time to take your meds."

"Pills, pills, pills. What would I do without them?"

"We don't want to find out." Kirsten waggled a finger at Cora. "They keep you in good shape."

"That's what you doctors and nurses keep telling me."

Kirsten grinned. "And we know what we're talking about."

Ian motioned toward Annie. "I'd like you to meet Kirsten Bailey. She's Adam's daughter and has recently come to work here after spending several years as a missionary nurse in Brazil."

Annie shook Kirsten's hand. "I'm glad to meet you."

"Nice to meet you, too. I hear congratulations are in order."

Annie nodded with that little smile curving her mouth. "It seems that news travels fast around here."

Kirsten laughed. "Yeah. It's like a small town. Everyone knows everyone else's business."

"That means we care about each other." Ian wondered how many people knew about his marriage to Annie. Probably more than he thought. Someone somewhere had probably figured it out or heard from some outside source about it. He had thought his secret was safe when she'd first arrived, but now he wasn't so sure.

Cora took her meds and handed Kirsten the empty cup. "That's for sure. I trip over my own two feet, and I barely arrived at the hospital before the prayer team."

"I'd say that's a good thing." Annie hugged Cora

again. "I know your prayers helped me. And I'm going to need them even more once Kara and Spencer get here."

"You can count on the seniors to pray for you." Cora pointed to the small chest next to the bed. "There's a photo album in the top drawer. I had Ruby and Liz bring that over for me because I was hoping you'd stop by today. I've got something to show you."

Ian went to the drawer and pulled out an album with a battered brown cover. "Is this it?"

Cora reached for it. "That's the one."

Annie looked over Cora's shoulder as she opened the album. "What do you want to show me?"

Cora thumbed through it. She stopped and patted her gnarled hand on one of the pages. "Remember me talking about my grandson? Here he is. Handsome, isn't he? His name's Brady Hewitt."

Annie nodded, and Ian leaned closer to get a look. Was Cora trying to fix Annie up with her grandson? Ian didn't like the idea much. He wasn't sure he wanted to work things out with Annie, but he didn't want anyone else to have an interest in her, either. Maybe it was time to decide what he wanted. Though the thought of making a decision gave him a headache.

"I raised Brady after my daughter was killed in a car accident and my son-in-law became so depressed he didn't take care of himself or Brady. I was a widow myself, so it wasn't easy trying to deal with my grandson, who was suffering from the loss of his parents, especially when he became a teenager."

"I'm so sorry to hear about your daughter. It must've been very difficult for both you and your grandson." Annie sat on the edge of Cora's bed as the older woman continued to talk.

"That boy took apart a motorcycle in my living room and ruined my carpet. I could've shot him, but I didn't want to serve time." Cora chuckled.

"I remember you said he was a good mechanic." Annie patted Cora's shoulder.

"Yeah, and I made him buy me a new carpet. That was the only thing good that came of it." Cora's expression saddened. "After that he left and dropped out of high school. I feel like I failed him, but I guess he's getting along okay. I haven't seen much of him in recent years. He calls every couple of months. Maybe I shouldn't have been so hard on him."

"You never know what's going to happen with kids. You do your best and pray." Ian thought about his own misguided youth. He'd had two parents who provided for his every need, but he'd chosen to rebel against their beliefs because he'd hated being a preacher's kid, expected to do the right thing all the time.

"I pray every day for him." Cora turned a page.

"I didn't bring the album out to talk about my grandson, but when I turned to his photo, I couldn't help myself. Anyway, I want you to look at this."

Ian leaned closer. "That's a nice-looking car. Is it yours?"

"Yes. I asked Brady if he wanted it, and he said no. My neighbor drives the car about once a week so the engine won't gum up. My house, which has been for sale since I moved here, finally sold. So that means I won't have a place to keep my car. I was going to sell it, too, but then I thought of you." Cora looked up at Annie. "I want you to have the car, so you have transportation to job interviews."

Annie shook her head. "But I can't afford to buy your car."

"Oh, I'm not asking you to buy it. I'm giving it to you."

Annie looked at Ian, then back at Cora. "That's too generous. I have to pay you something."

"No need. You'll be doing me a favor. I can't drive it anymore. If you take it, I won't have to pay for insurance or tags."

"But I will." Annie grimaced. "I'm sorry to be ungrateful, but I won't have any money until I find a more permanent job."

Ian wanted to help Annie, but he didn't want to discuss anything in front of Cora. "Annie, you should consider your options, then let Cora know what you want to do. You need a car, so you don't have to depend on others for a ride."

"You're right." Annie took a deep breath. "I'll let you know what I decide in a few days."

"Good." Cora nodded. "You're the perfect person for that car."

"Thanks for thinking of me."

"Now they better let me out of here in the morning."

"Let's pray about it." Ian reached for Cora's hand.

"Good idea." Cora took hold of his hand, a shimmer of tears in her eyes.

As he bowed his head, Annie held hands with Cora and slipped her other hand into his. He had to concentrate on the prayer not on his ex-wife or the way his heart skipped a beat as he held her hand. Ian swallowed hard, then gave thanks for all the good news of the day and prayed for Cora's quick recovery and wisdom for Annie. He silently prayed for wisdom of his own. He had to figure out what he wanted in regard to Annie.

When he said amen, Cora squeezed his hand. "Thanks so much."

"I'm glad we could visit, but we have to go." Ian wanted to talk to Annie alone so he could convince her to take the car and his help.

"Thanks for stopping by, and congratulations again, Annie. Let me know about that car." Cora waved her cane at Ian. "And don't you forget about dominoes."

"I'll be there." Ian waved as he escorted Annie from the room. When they were out in the hallway, he stopped. "It's nearly dinnertime. Let me take you out to eat?"

"Are you sure?" She gave him an impish smile.

If he hadn't counted to ten, the word *no* would have popped out of his mouth before he could think. But he had to convince her to take his help with the car expenses until she had some spare money. "Let's not analyze. I'm hungry, but if you'd rather not go, I'll walk you back to your apartment."

"Now that's what I call an enthusiastic invitation." She crossed her arms over her waist.

Her sarcasm wasn't lost on him. He didn't want to blow this opportunity. "I'd like to talk to you. Will you go out to eat with me?"

She smiled and slipped her arm through his. "I'd love to."

As Ian walked to his car with Annie clinging to his arm, he prayed. This was one of those times the book of Romans mentioned when the Spirit was making intercession by groaning because Ian had no idea how to pray.

The time he'd spent with Annie in recent weeks served to show him the changes she'd made in her life. She wasn't the same young woman who had tried to party her way to happiness. She had found delight in the Lord and helping here at The Village. Now she found joy at the prospect of having custody of her children again. What should be his part in all of this? And how would she feel if she ever learned the whole truth? The role he'd played in her and her children's lives, before Annie had shown up at The Village.

Ever since she'd presented him with her case, he'd been avoiding even thinking of the other reason he hadn't wanted to represent her. Guilt inundated him when he thought of Annie's battle for her children. No. He shouldn't have guilt over protecting those sweet little kids. He was right to have reported her to the Division of Family and Children Services after she had used the money he had given her for drugs instead her children.

What would Annie think if she knew?

Annie couldn't believe he was asking her to eat with him. They'd been together most of the day. All this closeness was making her want something she probably couldn't have—a do-over with Ian. He'd told her he wasn't even sure they could be friends. Had he changed his mind? Is that what he wanted to talk about? Did she dare ask him, or should she wait? Patience. She needed to practice patience.

"Where are we going?" She tried not to speculate about what he wanted to say.

"Your choice." He opened the car door for her.

Her heart fluttered as she scooted into the front passenger seat.

He drove toward the exit at the main gate of The Village. "Where to?"

She looked over at him as he waited to pull onto the main road. He was silhouetted against the sun that beamed through the tall pines on one side of the gate. Her heart fluttered again. Was she hoping for too much out of this dinner invitation? "Let's go to that place where we used to go when we were in high school."

"You mean McGurdy's Pizza?"

She smiled. "Yeah. That's the place."

Ian turned right, maneuvering into early-evening traffic. "It's still there, but I have no idea whether the pizza's still good or not." He glanced her way. "You do remember we're going to have pizza on Saturday night at my parents' house?"

"You used to say no one can have too much pizza." Annie wasn't sure what this trip down memory lane would bring, but she wanted to find out.

"You're right." Ian chuckled.

After Ian parked, Annie quickly exited the car. She wondered if he remembered that they'd gone here on their first date. Was it still a teenage hangout?

As they entered the restaurant, Annie noticed that little had changed. Wooden plank tables and benches comprised the booths that lined the walls. Smaller square tables surrounded by ladder-back chairs sat in the center of the large room. A hostess led them to a booth and left them with menus. Annie wondered whether Ian still like sausage and pepperoni pizza. She preferred a veggie pizza, so they'd often compromised with pepperoni and mushroom toppings.

He looked up from the menu. "Should we order our old compromise?"

"I'd like that." He remembered. Was that a good thing? Did it mean his thoughts were also on their failed relationship?

When the waitress appeared, they ordered their drinks and pizza. After she returned with their drinks, plates and utensils, Annie looked at Ian. "What did you want to talk about?"

"Cora's car. Annie, you shouldn't worry about those expenses. You need that car."

"Yes, I should. I can't spend money I don't have."

"But you'll have it. I can lend you money, and you can pay me back when you can."

She took a deep breath, not sure this was a good idea. She kept thinking about how she'd asked him for money for the kids, then used it to buy drugs. Who could forgive something like that? "I have lots of other expenses to deal with before I get a job. I have things to buy for Kara and Spencer. Like car seats."

"What good are car seats if you don't have a car?" Ian frowned. "I'm in no hurry for you to pay me back."

"They'll need car seats for any time I have to transport them in a car, no matter whose car it is. Like on Sunday when you're supposed to drive me to church and out to dinner with your parents. The kids will need car seats, and you don't have them in your car."

Ian nodded. "Shows you I don't know much about taking care of kids."

Before Annie could comment, the waitress brought their food. The aroma of the freshly made pizza made Annie's stomach growl. "Guess I'm as hungry as you are."

Ian chuckled. "Let's pray."

Annie bowed her head and listened to Ian's deep voice as he gave thanks for their meal. If they'd been in tune with God when they'd first started dating would things have turned out differently for them? She had to quit thinking about the past, because nothing could change it. But this place was all about the past. Why had she come here?

Ian picked up the server. "Hold up your plate, and I'll give you a slice."

"Thanks." More memories overloaded Annie's mind. They were reliving a small piece of the past. Thankfully, they wouldn't relive the whole awful thing.

As they ate in silence for a few moments, Annie tried to think about the future—the future with her kids. She was excited for them to see their room and play with the toys Doreen had given them. She prayed they wouldn't look at her as a stranger.

Ian polished off a slice of pizza in no time and helped himself to another one. "Now that you've been through rehab, have you ever thought of contacting your parents?"

The pizza curdled in Annie's stomach. She gritted her teeth, suppressing her hurt and anger. "Why should I do that? They didn't care about me when I was growing up. They didn't care when I messed up my life. They didn't care when I had kids or when they were taken away. They didn't care about the time I spent in rehab. Why would they care about me now?"

Ian didn't say anything for a few moments, his expression sympathetic. "I know you haven't been close with your parents, but it's still something to think about. They might like to get to know their grandchildren."

"I doubt it." Tears threatening, Annie didn't want to talk about her parents. "Your parents care about me more than mine ever did."

"To be honest, I had no idea how much my parents cared about you."

Closing her eyes to keep the tears at bay, Annie nodded. She took a shaky breath before looking at Ian. "Me, neither. Your mom's been wonderful to me."

"That's why you need to try to talk to your parents. You never know what might happen."

"Don't preach to me, Ian. You weren't exactly on great terms with your parents when you were younger."

"That's true, but I see how wrong that was. Ever since you've been back in my life, I've become closer to my parents, especially my dad."

"See. Being around me hasn't been all bad."

"Did I ever say it was?"

"You didn't have to. I could see it in your eyes."

"Annie, I don't know what I'm going to do with you."

Love me. The words sat on the tip of her tongue. She grabbed her slice of pizza and took a big bite in order to keep from saying them.

When Annie didn't say anything, Ian gave her a wry smile. "I don't know why I said that. Guess I never had lessons in how to deal with an ex-wife, but I'm here to help you. If you need help with your kids, I'll try to do whatever I can."

"Thanks. You're going above and beyond your duty."

"I'm part of The Village of Hope. The Village is here to support you."

"I appreciate the support." So he looked at it

as part of his job. It was nothing personal. She should've known.

What had she done—asking Ian to help with children who weren't his? How could she ask that of the man she'd betrayed? Was she hoping against hope that Ian could accept another man's children—that he could accept her back into his life? Why had Doreen bolstered the thoughts that Annie had been kicking around for days? He said he would help. She should be grateful.

"I also want to talk about reuniting you with Kara and Spencer. We haven't discussed the caseworker's plan."

"What is it? I have a hard time thinking positive things about that woman." Grimacing, Annie shrugged. "Guess she feels the same way about me."

"Don't worry. You're going to show her that you deserve to have your children. We'll be meeting in my office day after tomorrow. Would you like Melody to be there, too?"

Annie nodded. "If she could, that would be great."

"If you ask, I'm sure she will." Ian took another bite of his pizza.

Annie's appetite fled at the thought of facing that caseworker. Even though the woman wasn't anywhere near here, just the thought of her intimidating demeanor had Annie on edge. "I wish that caseworker didn't have to be there."

"Yeah, she seems a little stern, but she's only there to observe. She's not going to get involved in the transition."

"I hope you're right. If anything goes wrong, she'll be sure to make a note of it." Annie couldn't keep the bitterness out of her voice.

"That's okay. She can take all the notes she wants because I have confidence that most of them will be good."

"Just most?"

Ian stared at her. "Don't you think that's an accurate estimation?"

"Yeah. I'm sure the kids will have some anxiety and fears. I hope they don't cry." Annie didn't want to think about what might go wrong, but she had to face facts. Her children would probably look at her more as a stranger than their mother. She hadn't seen them much in the past year, but that's the way it had to be. The short-term rehabilitation programs hadn't worked for her. She always relapsed. She'd needed Pastor John's long-term program, and that meant limited contact with her kids. It was a trade-off she hoped would be for the best in the end.

"I still want you to take a loan for Cora's car. I expect you to say yes, but I'll give you a couple of days to realize you need to do this. And everything is going to be okay. You have a whole lot of people rooting for you, and with God on your side, who can be against you?"

"No one." Annie needed to remember that. Look forward, not back. She wished she could stamp that on her brain because she'd been doing too much looking back. Even tonight with Ian had been a look back. Starting tomorrow, her focus was going to be on the future.

Chapter Nine

Two days later Annie sat on one of the leather chairs in front of Ian's desk. The walls of his office seemed to close in on her as she twisted her hands in her lap. Why worry when you can pray? The title of a little tune her grandmother used to sing roamed through Annie's mind. The senior ladies had met to pray this morning. Cora was doing well. She'd been there for dominoes—an answer to prayer. The fact that Kara and Spencer would be here in a few minutes was an answer to prayer. So why was she doubting now?

Melody roamed over to the window. "Annie, they're here."

Annie raced to the window and watched as Kenneth and Tami Webster, the foster parents, got out of their car. They looked so put together—a perfect couple—the Barbie and Ken of foster parents. Annie didn't want to be jealous, but envy snaked into her brain.

The Websters opened the back doors and leaned inside. Kara emerged first, dressed in violet leggings with white polka dots. A top with flounces of purple netting on the bottom half completed her outfit. Her dark brown hair was pulled back on top with a hair band. She looked so grown-up today. She held Tami's hand as she skipped up the walk. In a second Spencer came into view dressed in dark pants and a stripped knit shirt. Kenneth tried to comb Spencer's unruly brown hair as he picked up the little boy and carried him.

The children looked so happy. The Websters had been wonderful foster parents, but would that make it hard for the children to leave them? Would they like their new home? Would they now be happy with her? Would they love her? Her heart pounded as the questions pranced through her mind. *Lord, let everything be okay.*

Annie looked over at Ian. "Should I stand closer to the door or stay here?"

Ian motioned to her. "Come stand by me. Take a deep breath."

Taking a deep breath might be calming, but standing next to Ian would not. Annie's leaden legs somehow propelled her across the room until she stood next to Ian's desk. He walked over and gave her shoulders a quick squeeze. Melody came to her other side and hugged her.

A knock sounded on the door. This was it. The moment she'd been waiting for had arrived.

"Come in." Ian's voice was calm and reserved.

The door swung open, and Kara sprinted across the room and threw herself into Annie's open arms. "Mommy, I get to stay with you."

Tears flowing down her cheeks, Annie embraced her daughter with all the love she was feeling. "Yes, you do."

Annie held Kara tight until she'd regained her composure. She looked over at Spencer, who still clung to Kenneth with what looked like a death grip. Annie's heart sank. How was she going to win her son over? Why did he hesitate when Kara had come to her with so much enthusiasm? Fear froze Annie's thoughts. She didn't know how to react. She stood there, her mind in a whirl until she saw the caseworker staring at her.

With a determination not to let that woman win, Annie took Kara's hand and walked over to where Kenneth stood while he held Spencer. "Hi, Spencer. I'm glad you're here."

Spencer didn't respond. He buried his head in the foster father's shoulder. When Kenneth tried to hold Spencer out to Annie, the little boy bellowed and clung harder. Kenneth grimaced as he looked at Annie. "I don't know why he's acting this way."

Annie said a silent prayer that her idea would

work. "I have a thought. Let's go to the library. I have some books set aside for the kids."

The entire group followed Annie down the hallway. Still praying, she asked the volunteer librarian for the books. Then she headed for the children's area, furnished with a small table and chairs painted in primary colors, along with a kid-sized chair that looked like a baseball glove and a little sofa covered in a zebra-striped fabric. She held the books on her lap as she sat on the sofa. She patted the seat beside her. "Kara, here."

Kara instantly hopped up onto the sofa. "Are you going to read us a story?"

Annie nodded and showed her daughter the books. "Which one would you like me to read?"

While Kara studied the books, Annie glanced over at Ian, who was nodding his approval as he leaned against the bookshelves. She didn't allow herself to look at Elena Lamb, who'd inspected Annie's apartment the day before. Although there was nothing about Annie's apartment that didn't pass inspection, the caseworker appeared to dislike almost everything Annie had done, or had it been her imagination? Elena was probably glaring at her right now.

Melody and Tami pulled up chairs from the adult section and sat down. Kenneth continued to stand and hold Spencer, who had looked up to see what his sister was doing.

Success? At least he wasn't crying anymore.

Kara handed Annie a book. "I want this one."

Annie took the book about a pigeon and a bus and began to read. Kara laughed as Annie put as much animation into her voice as she could muster. The sound of her daughter's laughter warmed Annie's heart. Now if only Spencer would join in the fun. As Annie finished the book, she glanced over at her son. Although he wasn't clinging to Kenneth as he had been before, the little boy still showed no interest in coming to her. Would another book help?

Annie looked at Kara. "Would you like to choose some books from the shelves?"

Kara jumped up. "Where do I look?"

Annie took Kara's hand and showed her the children's books. "Here."

While Kara took book after book off the shelf and examined them, Annie stood nearby. She looked over at Spencer. "Spencer, would you like to help Kara pick out some books?"

The little boy shook his head, but he didn't seem quite as attached to Kenneth. Annie wished she knew what to do. While she considered her options, Ian plucked a book from the shelf. Holding the book open, he moved closer to Spencer. The toddler looked at the book with interest as Ian turned the pages.

Kara scampered toward Ian. "I want to see the book, too."

"Okay." Ian hunkered down next to Kara. "My mom used to read this to me when I was your age."

As soon as Ian showed Kara the book, Spencer squirmed to get down. "The book is mine."

Ian stood. "Spencer, would you like to sit on the sofa with me while I read it?"

Spencer nodded, and Kenneth set the child on the floor. The children joined Ian as Annie gave up her spot, choosing to sit on the arm. Ian had saved the day. She could have leaned over and kissed him for more than one reason. He'd broken the ice with Spencer.

When Ian finished reading, he looked over at Annie. "Would you like to read another book?"

Annie wasn't sure. Would Spencer retreat if she took Ian's place? "Let's ask Kara and Spencer."

"What do you think, kids? Should your mom read another book?"

As Kara nodded, Spencer jumped up from the sofa and ran across the room. Annie's heart sank, but her fears were unfounded. Instead of heading toward Kenneth, the little boy grabbed a book from the table and brought it to Annie. "This one."

Kara reached across Ian and pulled Annie onto the love seat. Ian scooped Spencer into his lap. The four of them sat squished together. The cozy arrangement had Annie's heart racing. She took a calming breath before she started reading. Everything was going to be okay, at least, for now. She had the children's rapt attention as she read with pronounced expression—the way her grandma used to read.

When Annie finished, Spencer looked over at her. "Another one."

The room filled with laughter as Tami handed Annie another book. "They love to listen to stories. They love this one."

"Thanks." Annie took the book.

Spencer pointed to the cover. "He's a monster."

Annie smiled. "I think he's silly looking."

"Me, too." Kara giggled.

Annie finished the story and closed the book with satisfaction. "Okay, kids, would you like to see your room?"

"I do." Kara hopped up and tugged on Annie's arm.

Annie glanced around. "Should we walk or drive?"

"It's a beautiful afternoon. Let's walk." Melody headed for the door. "You can show the kids the fountain. It's decorated for a birthday."

Tami touched Annie's arm. "We have the children's things in our car. It's better if we drive over."

Elena stepped forward. "I'll show them where to go."

"Thanks." Annie forced herself to smile at the caseworker. When the woman returned the smile,

Annie almost let her jaw drop, but she smiled again instead.

"Everyone ready?" Ian opened the door.

"Let's see that fountain." Annie held out her hands to her children and prayed that they would grab hold. When they did, she breathed a sigh of relief.

Even though the children held her hands, Annie feared they might balk when the Websters headed to their car. Thankfully, Ian had their attention focused on the fountain where purple water bubbled from the top and cascaded down each tier. Purple balloons bobbed in the spring breeze.

"It's purple," Kara yelled. "Purple is my favorite color."

Smiling, Annie glanced down at her daughter. "I think I could tell that as soon as I saw you today. Your ruffles match the fountain."

Kara held out the flounces on her shirt. "I know. What's your favorite color?"

Annie wasn't sure. It had been a long time since she'd thought about something as simple as a favorite color. She'd been surviving, not really living. Today felt like she was living again. "Do you think my favorite color could be purple, too?"

Kara squinted up at Annie. "I guess it's okay if you have the same favorite color as me."

"Thanks." Annie gave Kara's hand a little squeeze. "Spencer, do you have a favorite color?"

"Boys don't have favorite colors." Kara wrinkled her nose. "But he loves his blue truck, so blue must be his favorite color."

Annie glanced over at Ian, who was walking on the other side of Spencer, just in time to see Ian stifle a laugh at Kara's know-it-all statement. "Spencer, is Kara right? Is blue your favorite color?"

"Orange. I like orange." Spencer looked up at her, his brown eyes wide. "Do you like orange?"

"Very much."

"But not as much as purple. It's a better color." Kara looked around Annie at her brother.

A little sibling rivalry couldn't hurt, could it? At least this was better than Spencer not wanting to have anything to do with her.

When they reached the fountain, the children raced around it as they watched the balloons dance in the sunlight. Stopping, Kara looked up at Annie. "Is it okay if I touch the water?"

"You can put a finger in it." Annie went over and placed her index finger in the water and pulled it out. She held up her finger. "It didn't turn purple."

"I wouldn't want a purple finger." Kara wrinkled her nose. "I can't reach."

"I'll lift you up." Annie put her arms around Kara.

"I wanna be up," Spencer bellowed.

"Sure, little buddy." Ian scooped Spencer up in

his arms and let him touch the highest level of the fountain. "Was that fun?"

Spencer nodded but squirmed to get down. Ian set the little boy on the ground and looked at Annie. "We'd better head to your place so we're there by the time the others arrive."

Ian looked down at Spencer. "How about a piggyback ride?"

"I want one, too." Kara pouted.

Annie glanced at Ian. "You take Kara, and I'll take Spencer since he's smaller."

"Good idea. What do you think, Kara?"

"That's good." Kara clapped her hands.

Ian put her on his back. "Hold tight while I help Spencer up."

After Spencer was settled on Annie's back, the foursome trotted across the quad to Annie's apartment building. In the distance, Elena and the Websters were waiting. Annie hoped the final transition would go well.

After everyone was in the apartment, Annie showed the children to their room. Kara raced to the bed with the pink coverlet and a purple stuffed bear gracing the pillow. Annie had forgotten about the purple bear. God must have been guiding her when she'd picked that out.

Kara hugged the bear and smiled up at Annie. "My favorite color."

In a moment of a panic, Annie searched the area

around Spencer's bed. Was there something orange on his side of the room? He would think she was playing favorites if he didn't find something orange. Then Annie spotted it. The orange foam ball sitting next to the blue-and-orange toy basketball hoop. She picked up the ball and handed it to the little boy. "Do you want to shoot a basket?"

Spencer grabbed the ball from Annie and stationed himself a few feet in front of the hoop. He threw the ball, and it went in. Applause filled the room. Spencer smiled and clapped, too. The adults laughed. Annie was feeling good. Why had she worried?

After the children had inspected the room and found a place for their belongings, they looked over the rest of the apartment. Finally, the moment of reckoning arrived. The Websters and the caseworker were ready to leave. Annie would be alone with her children for the first time in over a year. How would they react? How would she? The future stretched out ahead of her, and she didn't know what it held. Only God knew, and Annie was glad He was on her side.

Annie shook hands with the caseworker and the Websters and thanked them for caring for her children. She held her breath as the children gave hugs and goodbyes to their foster parents. She finally breathed when no tears or hysterics ensued. After giving Annie a hug, Melody left along with the other three.

Only Ian remained. He looked at her as the door closed. "Are you going to be okay?"

Annie nodded. "Absolutely."

"If you're good, I'll be going."

This was it. She was going to be on her own. That panicky feeling churned her stomach. "Thanks for everything. You've been a big help."

As Ian opened the door and stepped into the hall, he looked at her again. "You're sure you're okay? You look a little rattled."

Annie released a sigh and lowered her voice. "I'm a little nervous, but we'll be fine."

"If you need help, call me." He quietly closed the door behind him.

Annie turned to find the children staring at her. "Is everything okay?"

"I'm hungry." Kara wrinkled her nose, obviously her signature expression.

"Do you like hot dogs?" Both the children nodded, and Annie breathed another sigh of relief. "You can color at the table while I fix them."

"I don't like to color." Kara wrinkled her nose again.

"Oh, okay." Now what did she do with the kids while she tried to fix them a meal? "How about watching something on TV?"

"I like *Sofia*."

Annie only had basic cable in the apartment. She had a bad feeling that she didn't get the program Kara wanted. Why had she mentioned TV? Annie hunkered down in front of Kara. "I'm sorry, but my TV doesn't get *Sofia.* Let's go to your room and see if we can find some toys to play with until I get your food ready."

"I want to watch *Sofia,*" Kara bawled.

As Spencer started to wail, too, Annie counted to ten and prayed. "Not tonight. We'll see what we can do about it tomorrow. Okay?"

Kara scowled at Annie. "We had *Sofia* at Ms. Tami's house."

Annie forced herself to stay calm. "I'm sorry, but you'll have to do with what I have. Sit here on the sofa while I look for a game."

Not waiting for her daughter's response, Annie headed for the children's bedroom and quickly found a couple of electronic gadgets that Doreen had given her. The brightly colored games helped children learn letters, numbers and colors. As Annie came back down the hallway, she saw the kids sitting on the sofa, their little legs sticking straight out, their backs pressed against the sofa. They looked frightened. Annie's heart ached. She hadn't meant to scare them. Had her tone been harsh? She had to make it up to them. What would they tell the caseworker? Was she already making a mess of things?

Annie quickly sat between them and tried to make her voice cheerful as she turned on the games, their lights flashing. "See what I found. One for each of you."

Kara reached for the bigger one. "Ms. Tami had one like this. I like it."

Thank You, Lord. Annie glanced down at Spencer. He didn't seem to know what to do with his. She punched at couple of buttons, and the gadget played a catchy tune. "See what you can do with this?"

Finally, the children occupied themselves with the games, and Annie rushed to prepare the hot dogs and a microwave vegetable dish. She really needed those cooking lessons. The microwave beeped and Annie extracted the hot dogs and put in the vegetables. She put the hot dogs in buns and put them on plates. When the vegetables were done, she called the children to the table.

They settled in their seats as Annie put their plates in front of them. "Would you like ketchup with your hot dog?"

Both of the kids nodded, and Annie took the ketchup bottle and squirted some on their plates.

"That's not the way Ms. Tami does it. She puts it on the hot dog."

Annie was tired of hearing Ms. Tami this and Ms. Tami that. But maybe she should take a clue from Ms. Tami and do some of the things the other woman had done. After all, the children were used to that routine. It would probably make the transition easier. She had to remember to be grateful for the Websters, who had been willing to take in her children. For the most part, her kids were happy, and she owed this couple a debt of gratitude.

They managed to get through supper without another episode of discontent. They played with their games, and she played a short game of hide-and-seek with them. Spencer didn't exactly get the concept, but he had fun even though he chose the same hiding place every time.

An hour later with the children tucked into bed, Annie cleaned up the kitchen, then got dressed for bed. She couldn't believe how tired she was. She hadn't realized how much the emotions of the day had taken out of her. Slipping into bed, she reached for her Bible. She read the chapters on the reading list she had from her study group, then picked up the thriller she'd checked out from the library. Engrossed in the story, she jumped when she heard the click of the door. She looked up to find Kara standing in the doorway.

"Mommy, I can't sleep. Spencer is crying."

Annie's heart leaped into her throat as she launched herself out of bed and headed across the hall. The light coming through the doorway spotlighted Spencer sitting up in bed. Tears streaked his little face. He sobbed.

Annie sat on the bed beside him, worry crowding her mind. "Spencer, what's wrong?"

"I want my mommy."

"I'm here, Spencer. Mommy's here."

"I want Ms. Tami."

A pain she couldn't describe shot through Annie's heart. She wanted to cry, too. What was she going to do with Spencer? Annie picked Spencer up in her arms and held him close, rocking him back and forth. *Lord, please help me.*

"It's okay, Spencer. We're living with our real mommy now," Kara said.

Annie closed her eyes as she rocked Spencer and reached out to draw Kara close. "Thank you, sweet girl."

"Why are you thanking me, Mommy?"

"Because I love you." Annie's voice cracked. "I love you so much, and I'm glad you're here with me."

"Me, too." Kara snuggled closer, warming Annie's heart.

Annie rocked and rocked with Spencer until the little boy's sobs subsided. He snuggled close, and Annie's worry subsided, as well. When she finally heard his steady breathing, she managed to get him back into bed without waking him.

"Will Spencer stop crying now?" Kara looked up at Annie as she tucked the little girl into bed.

"He's sleeping, so we can hope so."

"If he starts crying again, should I come and get you?"

Annie nodded as she kissed Kara on the cheek and brushed back her hair from her face. "You're such a good big sister."

Kara smiled. "I am a good big sister."

"Good night, my sweet girl."

Annie stood in the doorway for a moment and looked at her children. Spencer slept soundly, and Kara closed her eyes. As Annie traipsed back to bed, she took in the reality of having her children back. This wasn't going to be easy if she was going to do it right. She definitely had to rely on God, and she thanked Him for giving her the support of the people here at The Village.

Tomorrow was an introduction to the day care here on campus. How would the kids deal with that? Could she help them cope with all the new things in their lives? She longed to have a partner to share this responsibility. She wanted to share her life with Ian again, but the same questions haunted her. Would they be good for each other? Could he forgive her completely? Would he be willing to take responsibility for another man's children? She still had no answers.

Chapter Ten

After Ian finished his talk and video presentation to his dad's congregation, he joined his dad on the front pew. He looked up to the stage where Annie was taking her place behind the pulpit. A chuckle emanated from the congregation as one of the elders gave her a box to stand on and adjusted the microphone to her petite height. Ian's heart beat in double time as he watched her. Every time he'd been with her in the past few days, he couldn't stop thinking about the possibility of a renewed relationship with her. Did he have a self-destructive wish?

Once Annie was settled, she looked out over the congregation. "My name is Annie, and I'm a recovering substance abuser. Ian has already talked to you today about the ministries of The Village of Hope. I'm here to put a face to one of those ministries. The women's ministry helps women in all kinds of circumstances—some who are fleeing

abuse and some like me who need help transition-
ing from a substance abuse program to a productive
life. The Village has provided housing, a temporary job and legal assistance in my quest to regain
custody of my children."

Annie paused and smiled. "I'm thrilled to report that my daughter and son are now a part of
my life again. Most importantly, The Village has
grounded me in the truth that faith in God will
guide me through good times and bad. They have
connected me with people who care what happens
to me. I urge you to consider supporting The Village through your prayers, volunteering and financial contributions. You will be giving a helping
hand to many like me."

Ian's admiration for Annie grew. He'd never
stood before a large crowd like this and admitted
his substance abuse. He'd done so in his small recovery group, but it never went beyond that. More
often than not he tried to hide his past rather than
show how God had changed his life. He could take
a lesson from Annie. She freely admitted that without God in her life she would never have overcome
her addictions. The same thing applied to him.

His dad leaned over. "She's come a long way.
Have you thought about—"

"Not now." Shaking his head, Ian turned away.

He tried to focus his attention on Annie's presentation, but his mind wandered back to the previous

evening at his parents' house. The children had devoured the pizza, and his mom had entertained the two youngsters in her playroom, thrilled to have little children about again. She hadn't given away all her toys, almost as if she expected to see Annie's children on a regular basis. His dad had even gotten down on the floor and helped Spencer build a tower with blocks.

The whole family-like atmosphere served to make Ian examine what he really wanted. He couldn't deny that he was falling in love again. There was no doubt about it. Did he have the courage to do something about it? He wasn't sure. His dad was sure to press for answers. Ian didn't miss the fact that his parents were campaigning to get Annie and him back together. Would it work this time?

He wanted to quit thinking about it, but with Annie standing before him the task was impossible. He glanced toward the other side of the auditorium. People appeared to be hanging on her every word. Not surprising since she was doing the same thing to him. Her charm and grace were winning hearts and minds for The Village of Hope's ministry. She was winning his heart and mind, too.

When Annie finished her short talk, she came and sat next to Ian. As his dad got up to give the sermon, Ian leaned over to Annie. "You did a great job."

"Thanks." She didn't look at him, but a smile curved her lips.

When the worship service was over, folks greeted Annie and told her how much her talk inspired them. As she took time to speak with each person, everything about her was engaging. He was losing his battle not to love her. Her life testified to the goodness of God.

She was no longer the girl who had let her parents' disinterest drive her toward a destructive lifestyle. He could still see the girl he had once loved—the one with the tender heart who had lost her beloved grandparents. She'd become a woman who knew God's grace and knew what she wanted from life. And he was afraid it didn't include him.

While Ian stood there trying to figure out his own feelings, his mother approached with Kara and Spencer in tow.

Kara bounded up to him and shoved a paper at him. "Hi, Mr. Ian. See what I made."

Ian inspected the paper with cotton balls glued all over it. "This must be a sheep."

Kara wrinkled her nose. "A lamb."

"Of course. A lamb." Ian glanced over at Annie, who was exclaiming over Spencer's paper. "Another masterpiece?"

Annie smiled at him. "Absolutely. Don't you know my children are brilliant?"

"Their mother is brilliant. Let me tell you again what a great job you did."

Doreen came up and put an arm around Annie's shoulders. "She did, didn't she? I'm so proud of you. The men who count the offering told me the special offering for The Village was close to five thousand dollars between the two services."

"That will definitely help with the finances, but we still have a ways to go."

"We're getting there little by little. Some of the permanent changes we've made will help the ministry going forward." Annie sounded more like a finance person than a former drug addict. "And we have more churches to talk to."

"But those congregations are much smaller than this one, so there won't be any five-thousand-dollar offerings." Ian could only hope for a small portion of that sum.

"God might surprise you." Annie gave him a speculative look.

"I'm hungry." Kara pulled on Annie's arm, interrupting the adult conversation.

"You're always hungry. Do you have a hollow leg?" Smiling down at her daughter, Annie poked at one of Kara's legs.

The little girl giggled. "You're silly, Mommy."

Annie's face brightened at the word *mommy*. She seemed to be getting along well, but he hadn't had a chance to talk to her and ask how things were going with the kids. Would she ask for help if she needed it, or would she be too proud to admit she needed assistance? The children seemed happy, and Annie seemed happy. So why should he worry about it? None of it should be his concern, but it was. He'd aided Annie in reuniting with her children. He had an obligation to see that it went well.

While they waited for his dad to finish greeting the folks who filed out of the auditorium, Annie fished in her purse and produced a bag of snacks that she passed out to Kara and Spencer. Then she turned to him and held up the bag. "Want some?"

For just an instant, the enticing tone of her voice and her expression took him back to the first time he'd experimented with drugs in the basement of her parents' home. Like in the story of Adam and Eve, he had followed the path of Adam and didn't resist the temptation. From that moment on, he was lost until an accident saved his life. He shook his head as he pushed the unpleasant memory away. "We'll be eating soon enough."

Annie smiled. "Okay, kids, let's go with Mr. Ian to the restaurant."

On the way, Ian listened to Kara and Spencer chatter about their Bible school classes. Annie was strangely silent. On Mother's Day was she thinking about her own mother or maybe her grandmother? He wanted to ask, but he was afraid the subject would make her sad. He wanted her to be happy whether her happiness included him or not.

After they were seated at their table, a server took their drink order and instructed them to help themselves to the buffet. Ian helped Annie get plates for the children. They returned to the table just as the server brought their drinks.

She put the drinks on the table. "You have a lovely family. Happy Mother's Day."

Annie looked at Ian with a grimace, and he decided there was no point in explaining to the server. He smiled and nodded.

"Thanks." Annie's voice squeaked. After the server was gone, she looked over at him again. "That was awkward."

"Don't worry about it. It was a natural mistake."

Before Annie could say anything else, Doreen and Jordan arrived.

"Can Ms. Doreen sit by me?" An imploring expression painted Kara's face.

"Sure I can." Doreen motioned for Ian to move over, and she slipped into the chair next to Kara. "What do you have to eat?"

As Kara listed the foods on her plate with great drama, Ian watched his dad helping Spencer. His parents and Annie's children had adopted each other right from the beginning. He hoped it was a good thing. During the meal, they talked and laughed like the real family the server had mistaken them for.

Before they headed to the dessert portion of the buffet, Jordan tapped his glass to get everyone's attention. "I want to wish Happy Mother's Day to these two lovely ladies." He gave Doreen and Annie cards and gifts.

Annie thanked Jordan for the book and gift card to a big-box store, and Doreen hugged her husband after she found a spa certificate inside of her book. Ian handed a card to his mother that contained a gift certificate to her favorite shop as he gave her a kiss on the cheek.

But he hadn't thought of getting anything for Annie, not even a card. Why had he been so stupid? Maybe he was having a hard time thinking of her as a mother. For most of the days since she'd reappeared in his life, she'd been without children. That was his only excuse.

Doreen fished in her purse and produced a couple of cards that she handed to Annie. "Some children were very busy at day care on Friday. I stopped by to be sure I got these before they were lost."

As Annie took the cards an expression of awe spread across her features. She opened the envelopes and carefully extracted the handmade cards. Her eyes filled with tears as she gazed at the simple pictures on the front and the little handprints on the inside. Wiping away the tears that trickled down her cheeks, she hugged Kara and Spencer. "Thank you so much. These are awesome. This is the best Mother's Day ever."

Despite his neglect, without a doubt for Annie the statement was true. She had her children back. That made for a perfect day. Could this new life she was building for herself ever include him?

Clutching her cards and book in one hand and holding Kara's with the other, Annie followed Ian as he carried Spencer to his car. Today was a Mother's Day to remember—the best Mother's Day of her life. She was clean and sober, and she had her children.

As they buckled the kids into their car seats, Annie wondered whether Ian resented having to cart her around. Did he view her as an obligation he couldn't disregard? She hated the thought of being someone's obligation, especially Ian's.

After they were settled in the car, Ian glanced at her as he pulled out of the parking lot. "When we get back to your place, will you have time to talk to me, or will you be busy with the kids?"

She studied his expression as he drove along the main road back to The Village. What did he want to talk about that he couldn't do here in the car? "The kids have a rest time in the afternoon, so we should be able to talk."

A few minutes later Ian pulled into the parking

lot near her building. They unbuckled the kids, and Ian again carried Spencer, who was nearly asleep already. Annie put Kara in her own bedroom with some books and puzzles so she wouldn't disturb Spencer, who went to sleep almost as soon as she put him into his bed.

When both kids were settled, Annie joined Ian in the living room. "What do you have to say?"

"I want you to have this." Standing, Ian brought an envelope out of his pocket and held it out. "I won't take no for an answer."

Annie took the envelope. She opened it and pulled out a check for an amount that would cover the expenses involved with getting Cora's car. "I can't—"

"Yes, you can, and you will." Ian stepped closer. "I didn't get you anything for Mother's Day. I feel bad about that."

"You shouldn't feel bad. I'm not your mother. I'm not your wife anymore, and we don't have children together. So I didn't expect you to get me anything. And just because you feel bad doesn't mean you should give me this." She waved the check in the air.

"You can pay me back when you're able. Take it." Ian's gaze didn't waver as he stared at her. "Cora doesn't want the bother of selling that car. Do it for Cora."

Annie wondered why she was fighting with Ian

over this. She needed a car. Was it her pride or something she couldn't define? She already owed him so much. She didn't want to owe him more. She released a heavy sigh. "Okay. I'll do it for Cora."

"Thank you." Ian smiled. "How's everything going?"

Annie wondered whether she should share her anxieties with Ian. Would he think she wasn't doing a good job and wish he hadn't helped her reunite with her children? Today was the best day so far, but things were far from perfect. "Let's sit down instead of standing here while we talk."

Ian smiled. "I was waiting for an invitation to sit."

Annie grimaced. "I'm sorry. I forgot my manners."

Ian plopped onto the sofa. "I was only kidding."

Annie frowned as she sat on the nearby chair. She thought a little distance between them would help keep her romantic thoughts in check. His kind gestures of the past few days had planted too much hope for reconciliation in her heart, and she couldn't let it get out of hand. "Don't tease me."

He chuckled. "You were always fun to tease."

"Did we have fun together?" The question came out of her mouth before she thought about the wisdom of the inquiry. It wasn't good to go there— back to the days when they were together.

Ian nodded. "I think before the alcohol and drugs took over our lives."

"I'm sorry I brought up the past." Annie shook her head. "We don't need to talk about it."

"There's still something from your past that we need to talk about. Let me have my say before you dismiss it again."

"What?" Annie was pretty sure she didn't want to hear what he had to say.

"While we were at the restaurant I was thinking about how you should visit your parents." Ian held up a hand. "I know you were angry with me for bringing this up before, but it's something you need to do if you really want to leave your past behind and move on with this new life. I'll watch Kara and Spencer when you go."

Annie nodded, knowing Ian was right. Last night's Bible reading for her study group had been about forgiveness. The scripture had put the topic front and center in her mind. She wanted Ian's forgiveness, and how could she expect that when she was unwilling to forgive her parents? Maybe reconciliation with her parents could be a precursor to reconciliation with Ian. She could only hope. "I won't argue. I realize it's something I need to do, but it won't be easy."

"I won't try to convince you otherwise. Forgiving is never easy."

"Is that the way you feel about forgiving me?"

He nodded and motioned to her. "Come sit by me."

Annie swallowed hard as she joined him on the sofa. Her heart pounded. What was he going to say? Besides the forgiveness, she longed to hear him say he still loved her. That wasn't going to happen, so why couldn't she stop thinking about it?

"I've struggled with forgiving you. That's why I know it's so important for you do this." He looked her in the eye. "I told you before I was working on this, and I need to say it to you. I forgive you, Annie. Forgive me for taking so long to tell you."

She wanted to throw her arms around him and tell him not only did she forgive him but that she loved him and wanted to start over. Instead, she smiled. "Thank you. I needed to hear that. And you don't have anything to be sorry for."

He smiled wryly. "You asked about being friends. I'd like to try that. What do you think?"

Annie nodded, afraid to say anything for fear her voice would crack with emotion. She wanted so much more than friendship, but friendship was a beginning. Maybe that's what they needed. Any reconciliation required a new start and what better start than as friends? She couldn't make Ian love her, but she could be the best friend he ever had.

Ian gave her a speculative look. "Okay, now back to my earlier question. Is everything good with you and the kids?"

If she wanted friendship with Ian, she was going to have to be completely honest with him. "It's a mixed bag. Today was a wonderful day, but the first night was miserable."

Ian frowned. "What happened?"

Annie didn't want to relive that night, but she told Ian about Spencer's problems going to sleep and the constant reminders that she didn't do things like Ms. Tami did. "Tami gave me a very detailed report about what she'd been doing with the kids and explained their regular routine. I didn't have a chance to read it that first night, but I've gone over it now. Things are better."

"They'll continue to get better."

"The day care workers hope so. Spencer was not happy at day care on Friday. He cried most of the day."

Ian shook his head. "But he was so happy Saturday night and today."

"I know. He loves your dad."

"The feeling appears to be mutual." Ian sat forward. "Do you think the kids are ready for me to babysit?"

Annie couldn't help smiling at Ian's concern. "Are you worried about them or you?"

"Both." His eyebrows knit together. "You know I haven't had much experience with kids. I might see my nieces and nephews three times a year at the most."

"Are you trying to back out on your offer to babysit?"

"No, I want you to talk to your parents. The kids and I will survive. I'll bribe them with pizza. They seemed to have inherited a love for pizza from their mother."

Annie laughed. "What time can you get here?"

"You can go right after you finish your work with the finances if you want. I'll pick up the kids from day care and bring them home."

Annie pressed her lips together. Was that a good idea? Would they balk at being picked up by someone other than her when this routine had just begun? There were so many unknowns. "Before we make any decisions, let's talk to the kids when they get up. If we let them be part of the decision, hopefully, you won't have crying kids on your hands."

"Okay, we'll see what happens when we talk to them."

Annie stared at Ian. Did that mean he intended to stay until they got up from their naps? How was she going to survive this much time alone with him? She wanted a new start with Ian—one that was based on the right things. She should use this time to work toward that goal. "Can you answer a question?"

"I'll try."

"You said the offering we got this morning for The Village would help, but that we have a ways to go." Annie paused, almost afraid to ask the question. "Does that mean the board might still shut down the ministry?"

"Don't worry, Annie. We're going to make it."

"You didn't answer my question. I don't want to lose my apartment and have to move the kids again. They've had enough upheaval in their lives."

"We're doing everything we can to make sure that doesn't happen."

"I'm sorry your mother roped you into babysitting for the cooking lessons, too."

"Honestly, I don't mind. I like your kids."

Ian's statement warmed Annie's heart, but she still didn't want to wear out her welcome in Ian's life. "I hope you're still saying that after you actually take care of them."

"I'm going to get a lot of practice." Ian chuckled. "Since I've been so busy with my legal work, tell me what's happening with your work on the finances."

"I like it a lot. I'm so thankful for this second chance to make something of my life." Annie sighed.

He nodded. "I believe you deserve a second chance. I got mine. Now you can have yours, too."

"I appreciate that." What could she possibly talk about to fill this time? Their past was a no-no subject. Too many reminders of the decadent things they'd done. *Keep it in the present.* "Tell me about being a lawyer for The Village."

"Sure. Sometimes it's routine, and other times it's a challenge, but whatever the case, I like helping people who have no other legal resources."

"Like me?"

Ian nodded. "Folks come here for all kinds of legal advice, including child custody and support, divorce, landlord-tenant problems, employment discrimination, foreclosure defense, veterans rights and domestic abuse. Just to name a few. I spend time giving folks advice on contracts, and I may refer them to other attorneys who do pro bono work because they may be more knowledgeable in a certain field than I am."

"Like you did with me?"

Ian gave her a wry smile. "Well, yours was a special case."

"Yeah, I guess so." So it wasn't only her case he had referred to someone else. Should that make her feel any better? Silly question. She was learning that he did what was in the best interest of the person he was trying to help. He was a good man—a wonderful man.

"I especially like to help elderly folks on fixed incomes who need legal advice. They often don't understand contracts or their rights in certain instances. They need an advocate."

"People like Cora?"

Ian nodded again as he continued to expound on his work. Annie understood more and more about him—the man he'd become since turning his life over to God. As much as she'd loved him before, she loved him even more now. Why had she left him? She hadn't been in her right mind. The decisions she'd made back then had been about her addictions.

"So what are your favorite TV shows?" Ian asked.

Annie shrugged. "I don't watch much TV. If it's on, something the kids like is usually playing. Maybe I should say my favorites are anything the kids will watch."

"That reminds me of the time I was visiting one of my brothers, and I walked into their TV room and found him watching some kid program—not a kid in sight. He said he was so used to watching kid TV that he didn't realize the absence of kids." Ian chuckled. "How about books—what do you like to read these days?"

"Suspense and thrillers."

Ian smiled. "Me, too, but that's not what you used to read. I thought you liked sci-fi."

"Yeah, that's when I was trying to escape the real world." Annie shrugged. "I've quit running away."

As Ian went on to mention his favorite authors, Annie didn't know what to make of his congenial conversation or his reason for staying till the kids got up. When she first came to The Village, he'd done his best to avoid her. What had changed?

No. She couldn't let herself hope that this conversation or his forgiveness had brought about other feelings for her. She wanted to be his best friend, but how did she accomplish that? The people she'd considered friends through the years had been people she'd partied with. Maybe she wasn't so good at friendship, but she was going to make an effort to learn what it meant to be a good friend.

While she made these plans about Ian and her, she had to remember that God's plan was the best plan. She hated to think that God didn't want them to reconcile, but she had to be prepared to accept that possibility.

Annie glanced toward the bedrooms. "Let me check on the kids. I know Spencer was asleep, but Kara wasn't, and it's all too quiet."

Ian chuckled. "Yeah, I learned from my brothers that quiet and kids are often not so good."

Annie tiptoed down the hallway and discovered Spencer still asleep and Kara snoozing on top of a book. Annie's heart tripped at the sight. Her babies were worn-out from a jam-packed Mother's Day. She prayed there would be many more wonderful days ahead for them. With the kids still asleep, what was she going to do with Ian?

Bridge. The thought struck her as she traipsed back to the living room. Would Ian go for some lessons? One way to find out. "Spencer's still asleep, and Kara fell asleep, too. Since we have time, how about bridge lessons?"

"How? The game needs four players."

"We'll lay out cards like they do in the bridge column in the newspaper."

Ian knit his eyebrows. "They have bridge columns in the newspaper?"

"Yeah, my grandma used to go over them with me."

"Is that how she taught you?"

"Actually, she and my grandpa had me play with one of their friends. She had this tablecloth with the bidding rules on it, and I used it to bid. They dealt the cards and let me sink or swim."

Ian chuckled. "Is that what you're going to do with me?"

"No, I used one of the library computers to get some stuff off the internet." Annie went to the drawer in nearby end table and pulled out a few papers held together with a paper clip. "Here they are."

He took the papers and leafed through them. "So you've been lying in wait for me with your bridge rules?"

"You don't have to do this, but Cora asks if you're afraid to show up at bridge as well as dominoes."

"You're so easy to tease." He tried to keep a straight face but finally burst out laughing. "Okay, show me how to play this game."

"I'll ignore your laughter." Annie sat cross-legged on the floor on the other side of the coffee table and dealt out the cards faceup as she explained what constituted a game in the major and minor suits.

"Laughter is good for your health." Ian also sat on the floor on the other side of the table and leaned against the sofa.

"Let's see if you're laughing when I finish with you." She gave him a lopsided grin, then proceeded to have him figure out what he would bid in each case.

He studied the rules and made a bid. Then they worked their way around the table playing the hands. After a half hour of practice, Ian had grasped the basics. She had always admired his intelligence. She should've known he would easily pick up the game.

Annie gathered the cards as she stood. "Are you ready to take on Cora and Ruby?"

"What do you think?" Ian sat on the sofa.

"Only one way to find out. Play against them." Annie put the cards in the end table drawer.

"Tuesday night?"

"It's a date."

Annie's heart fluttered as she sat in the nearby chair. Was it a date or only an expression? Better not to read anything into it. "I'll see you at the senior center, then."

"You have someone to watch the kids?"

Annie nodded. "Julie, my neighbor, said she'd watch them since I watched hers while she was studying for exams when I first came here."

"Good."

"Mommy, what's Mr. Ian still doing here?"

Annie turned at the sound of Kara's voice. "We've been talking."

"That's not fun." Kara wrinkled her nose.

Ian chuckled. "Grown-ups like to talk."

Spencer toddled into the living room, his hair sticking up in a dozen directions. He rubbed his eyes as he settled onto Annie's lap. "Looks like someone isn't quite awake yet."

Ian leaned over and tousled Spencer unruly hair. "What do you think, Spencer? Would you like me to pick you up from day care tomorrow so your mom can run an errand?"

"I would. I would." Kara jumped up and down.

"One vote in my favor."

Spencer scrambled up from Annie's lap. "Me, too."

"Two votes." Ian stood. "Looks like it's a go for tomorrow."

"Are you leaving?" Kara asked.

Ian nodded. "Yeah. I wanted to talk to you about tomorrow, but I have some work to do."

"Ah. I wish you could stay." Kara stuck out her lower lip.

"I'll see you tomorrow." Ian headed for the door.

Annie followed with Kara and Spencer close behind. "Thanks for everything today."

"Thanks for the bridge lessons. I think." Ian winked as he opened the door. "Bye. See you tomorrow."

"Bye." Annie's pulse skittered as she watched him go. He was so good with the kids. So good with her. Was it too much to hope that Ian could love her again? That they could be a family?

Chapter Eleven

On Monday after her finance work, with her kids safely under Ian's care, Annie drove to her parents' home in a suburban Atlanta neighborhood. She couldn't remember the last time she'd been there. As she approached the two-story brick house nestled on a wooded lot, she prayed even though she wasn't sure what to pray for. Her parents had disowned her. They'd seen Kara once and didn't know Spencer. Would grandchildren soften her parents' hearts?

Annie parked her car in the drive. Holding on to the steering wheel, she sat there for a few minutes and said another prayer. *Lord, give me Your peace no matter how my parents react to my visit.*

Annie took a deep breath as she rang the doorbell. Her pulse pounded all over her body as she waited for someone to answer the door. For a moment, she hoped no one was home. When the door opened, Marcia Payton stood there still dressed in her business suit, her dark hair coiffed to perfection. The only thing missing was her business smile.

"What are you doing here, Annie?" Marcia said, her expression unwelcoming.

Annie swallowed the lump in her throat. "I was hoping we could talk."

Marcia narrowed her gaze. "If you're here to ask for money, we have nothing to talk about."

Her mother's response was not unexpected, but it still pierced Annie's heart. She had brought this reaction on herself, but she wanted to show her mother the new Annie. Would her mother listen? "I'm not here about money. I have Kara and Spencer back, and I thought you might like to meet your grandchildren."

"If that's what you want, I suppose you can come in." Marcia stepped aside.

As Annie glanced around she realized her mother had done a complete renovation of the decor. "I like what you've done."

"Thanks." Her mother actually smiled.

"Who's at the door?" Richard Payton's voice boomed from the back of the house.

Annie swallowed hard as her father appeared in the front hall.

Marcia looked back. "Annie's here."

Richard charged toward the door waving a hand

in the air. "What do you think you're doing coming here? I won't have a drunk and drug addict in my house. Get out."

Marcia put a hand on her husband's arm. "Richard, please. She's sober—"

"Don't try to defend her. She's brought nothing but trouble on herself and this family. She doesn't belong here." Richard turned and glared at Annie as he shook a finger at her. "Get out of here. I don't want to see you again."

Annie blinked and pressed her lips together, trying hard not to let her father's angry tones make her cry. She gathered her courage. "Dad, I'm sorry you feel that way. I've changed—"

Richard opened the door. "That's what you want us to believe, but we know you always slip back into your old ways. If you don't leave, I'll call the police."

Annie looked over at her mother, but Annie would get no help from that corner. Her father had always intimidated even her usually strong-willed mother. Annie cast one last glance in her mother's direction and read the sadness in her eyes. Forcing herself not to run, Annie walked to her car with her head held high. She backed out of the driveway and drove away without giving in to the urge to look back. She would not give her father the satisfaction.

A block away, she pulled the car to the curb, laid her forehead against the steering wheel and sobbed.

She'd had such high hopes that her parents would want to get to know their grandchildren. Instead, they wanted nothing to do with any of them. When she returned home, Ian would ask what happened. How could she possibly tell him?

Ian's first experience with babysitting was going well. He'd picked up Kara and Spencer from day care without any problem. They had seemed eager to go with him, especially when he suggested they visit Ms. Cora. The kids had been a hit with the seniors when Annie and he had taken them for a visit. With each passing day, Annie and her children were more a part of his life than he'd ever imagined.

After Ian and the children visited the assisted-living center, they had headed to Annie's apartment. He'd placed an order for their pizzas while visiting the seniors and it arrived just minutes after they got to the apartment. He congratulated himself on heads-up thinking. The kids ate their pizza like champs, but Spencer had more sauce on his face than he did in his stomach.

After they ate and the last dish was in the dishwasher and the last crumb wiped from the table, Ian escorted the kids into the living room. What did he do with them now? Play games?

Kara quickly rescued him. "Mommy always reads us stories after we eat. Will you read to us?'

"Sure. Get your books."

Kara raced away with Spencer trailing behind. She returned with a stack of books that she could barely carry. Had Annie checked out the whole children's section from the library?

The little girl held out a book to him. "Read this one first."

Ian recognized it as one Annie had read during the transitional meeting. He remembered how she'd read with so much expression. He didn't think he could come close to her flair for reading, but he would give it his best shot. "You like this story?"

Kara nodded. "So does Spencer. He laughs when Mommy reads it."

Ian grimaced. He had a tough act to follow. "Okay, kids, up on the sofa."

With the children on either side of him, Ian read the book about the pigeon and the bus and considered it a moderate success when Spencer let out a little laugh. Then Kara handed him another book from the stack. He wondered whether he would get through the books before Annie returned.

Kara snuggled close as Ian read more books. When he finished the sixth book, she looked up at him with her sweet little smile and eyes so much like Annie's. "I like it when you read books to us. Could you be our daddy, because me and Spencer don't have one?"

Kara might as well have punched Ian in the gut.

Her question took the breath right out of him. How could he answer? Could he make things work with Annie again? Could she love him? He didn't want to encourage a little girl's hope or put unattainable dreams in her heart, but he didn't want to make her feel unwanted. Did he have the courage for a little girl's sake to talk to Annie about where they might fit into each other's future? But how could he move forward with her when he'd been the one to report her to DFCS?

His niggling doubts about whether Annie could follow through, his fear of being rejected and hurt again and his lack of courage kept him from broaching the subject. They'd established a tentative friendship. Shouldn't he leave it at that?

So what was he going to say? This was not the kind of trouble he'd anticipated when he'd agreed to watch Annie's kids. While he tried to come up with something to say, the door opened. Annie walked into the apartment, and the kids jumped up to greet her. Saved by Annie's return.

Hunkering down, she hugged them. They talked over each other as they told her about their evening. She looked at him over the tops of their heads and smiled. His heart bumped against his ribs. Despite her smile, he was pretty sure she'd been crying. Her visit must not have gone well.

She stood. "Will you help me put the kids to bed, then we can talk?"

"Sure." He followed her back to the children's bedroom.

After the kids said their prayers and Annie tucked them into bed, Ian went out to the living room with Annie. "So what happened?"

Closing her eyes, she pressed her fingertips to her mouth. Finally she dropped her hand to her side. "I can't talk about it right now. Tell me how you and the kids got along."

Ian wished he could take away the hurt in Annie's eyes. Maybe honoring her request not to talk about it was the best thing he could do. Should he try to lighten her mood with a few quips about her kids, or would that make her feel worse? "The evening went pretty well. The pizza was a hit, but you should've seen Spencer. He had sauce all over his face."

"You did a good job cleaning him up." Annie gave him a hesitant smile as they stood facing each other in the center of the living room.

She was putting on a brave face, and that soft spot for her in his heart grew wider. He swallowed hard. "Are you ready to talk about seeing your parents?"

She pressed her lips together and closed her eyes. When she finally opened them, she took a deep breath. "It didn't go well. I barely made it past the door. As soon as my father saw me, he started to yell, while my mom stood there, just looking at me like I had two heads. They hate me."

"How could anyone hate you?"

"Didn't you hate me?"

Ian placed his hands on Annie's shoulders. "I've never hated you, Annie. You hurt me. You made me very angry, but I never hated you."

Tears streamed down Annie's cheeks. "I'm so sorry. I've hurt everyone."

"You know I've forgiven you." Ian wiped Annie's tears with his thumb. She looked up at him as a sob escaped. He pulled her into his arms and held her. Unlike that day in court when she'd hugged him with thankfulness, tonight she needed comfort. He wanted to give her comfort, but he didn't know how to take away her sorrow.

He stepped back for a moment and gazed down at her tear-streaked face. There was only one thing he wanted to do. He pulled her into his arms again and kissed her. Nothing in the world mattered except Annie. She clung to him. He deepened the kiss. All his renewed feelings for the woman who had once been his wife bubbled up in that kiss. Then he came to his senses. He couldn't let this happen.

He ended the kiss and stepped back so fast that he almost stumbled over his own feet. He held up his hands. "I shouldn't have done that. I'd better go."

Annie stared at him. "Don't leave without talking about this. You can't just kiss me and run out. I thought we were friends."

Ian gazed at the floor, afraid to look her in the eye. "That kiss wasn't about being friends. It wasn't right. My thoughts weren't right. I can't stay. Good night, Annie."

Ian rushed out of the apartment. He didn't want to leave her without a better explanation. He'd abandoned her when she was hurting, but he was afraid to stay. Afraid he would have hurt her more if he had stayed. She'd responded to his kiss in the most inviting way. The attraction between them was as fresh as those early days of their relationship.

The kiss had shaken him to his very core. All the years he'd spent loving her, and all the years he'd spent trying to forget her, had come rushing back at him like a huge tidal wave. One kiss had opened up his heart, and the gamut of emotions he'd bottled up inside for too long had poured over him. How could he deal with the mix of feelings? Hurt. Guilt. Anger. Love.

Love.

Yes, love. He'd been trying to run from it, but he couldn't deny it any longer. But he wasn't ready yet to face the reality of his feelings for Annie.

Their love had brought them both a lot of heart-ache. Could things be different now?

The following Thursday Annie headed to the store, where she hoped to quickly pick up a few groceries. She wanted to have Kara and Spencer ready for bed by the time Ian came to babysit. How would Ian act tonight after the way he'd left on Monday? He hadn't backed out of babysitting, so she could take her cooking lesson from his mother. Annie was grateful for that.

Annie remembered his kiss. She'd wanted more, and he wouldn't talk about it. Where did that leave them? What did it mean that he had practically run out of her apartment? Was he running from his feelings, or had he decided they could never recapture the love they'd once shared?

Lost in her thoughts, Annie walked across the parking lot, the staccato tap of her heels accenting the buzz of rush-hour traffic on the nearby street. The heat from the day radiated off the blacktop.

"Well, well, well. If it isn't my Annie Payton."

Annie jerked her head up at the sound of the familiar voice. "What are you doing here, Jesse?"

"I'm here to check on you. I saw you out with your do-gooder ex-husband. Trying to take him down again?" The sneer on Jesse's face curdled Annie's stomach.

"He's twice the man you'll ever be. Go away,

Jesse." Annie's stomach churned as she looked at his disheveled appearance. Is that what she used to look like?

He laughed, his breath reeking of alcohol. He moved closer and grabbed her arm. "That's not what you used to say. How about you and me going out to party tonight? Remember the good times we used to have?"

She jerked away. How had she ever lived with Jesse? How had she allowed herself to be a smelly drunk like him? She gritted her teeth. "If you don't leave now, I'm going to scream. I'll call the police. Get away from me."

He took a step back but stared at her with those bloodshot brown eyes. "I have rights. I want to see my kids."

"You've had plenty of time to see your kids, but you never did. You never paid a cent to support them. If I have my way, they'll never know you exist." Annie prayed he'd go away. She hoped he couldn't see how much her legs trembled.

"Give me some money, and I won't bother you again."

"I don't have money to give you. Even if I did I wouldn't give you anything. Get out of here before I scream." Annie saw a couple approaching from the far end of the parking lot. Jesse had seen them, too.

"This isn't the last you've heard of me. I'll be

back." He turned and staggered across the parking lot.

Shaking, Annie leaned against a nearby car and took several deep breaths. How had he found her? When had he seen her with Ian? Was he stalking her? The questions rifled through her brain. She didn't want to wind up like the women in her study group who had fled from men who stalked and abused them. Jesse had never scared her before, but now he did.

When she regained her composure, she drove back to The Village. She'd been so rattled and wanted to get away from there so fast that she'd forgotten to go into the store. Should she tell someone about this? What would Ian think if he found out? Annie definitely didn't want her caseworker to get wind of the incident. The woman seemed to have it in for her and would probably use it to show the court that she wasn't a fit mother. Annie couldn't let that happen. Despite her fear of Jesse, she would have to keep this incident to herself.

Jesse was a drunk. He only wanted money so he could buy more booze. Annie remembered being desperate like that. She tried to shake the awful image away—the image of her stealing from Ian. Jesse was a reflection of what Annie used to be. Stopping at the traffic light, she put her hand over her mouth to stifle a sob. She could hardly wait to hug her kids.

* * *

Ian punched in the code to enter Annie's apartment building. He took a deep breath and slowly released it as he knocked on her door. He wasn't sure how she would receive him since he'd run away after kissing her. He wasn't sure how to deal with the situation, so he'd decided to take the coward's way out and say nothing. He would pretend nothing had happened, and he hoped she would leave as soon as she gave him the instructions regarding her kids.

When the door opened, Kara and Spencer enveloped him in hugs before Annie could say hello. At least the kids were glad to see him. He hoped that boded well for the evening. He nodded to Annie as he laid his book on the coffee table and scooped the kids up, one under each arm and trotted around the living room while the kids giggled.

"I hope you know what you're doing." Annie stood there with her hands on her hips and irritation on her face.

Ian stopped and deposited the kids, who were already in their pajamas, on the sofa. "We were having a little fun."

"Don't get them too riled up or they won't go to sleep." She pointed to a paper on the coffee table. "Instructions for tonight. Call me if you have a problem. I'm off."

"Don't burn anything." He grinned, hoping to make the moment light.

She gave him an annoyed look. "Your smart-aleck remarks won't win you any prizes."

"But my great babysitting talents will." He still hoped to get a smile out of her. What was he thinking? He'd hoped she would leave as soon as he stepped inside. Now he was trying to flirt with her. He was a mess.

"I wouldn't count on that, either." She bent down and gave Kara and Spencer each a hug and kiss. "Kids, please be good for Mr. Ian and do what he says."

"I'm sure they will."

Without another word, she left.

She was obviously as eager to get away as he'd hoped she would be when he'd arrived, but now that she was gone he wished she'd come back. He should be thankful, because being with her brought back all the feelings from Monday night. That had been a disaster. Why had he succumbed to the temptation to kiss her? It couldn't be undone, so he shouldn't think about it. But he couldn't forget, and he couldn't let it happen again.

A little hand tugged on his arm. He looked down. Kara stared up at him. Some babysitter he was. He'd almost forgotten the kids. "Is it games or books tonight?"

"Books." Kara raced away to her room again as she'd done on Monday night.

Ian picked up the instructions Annie had left. Even looking at her perfect handwriting had him thinking about stuff he shouldn't be thinking about. This whole scenario fit the Apostle Paul's words in Romans. "I do not understand what I do. For what I want to do I do not do, but what I hate I do." If there ever was a scripture that fit him, this was it.

He released a harsh breath determined to concentrate on two small children instead of one petite woman. He studied the instructions. Story time. Brush teeth. Prayers. Bedtime. He could handle this.

Kara came back into the room with her stack of books. This time she placed them on the coffee table, then hopped up on the sofa. "You pick the first book."

Was this a test? Would she be happy with his choice? He shook his head as he grabbed a book. Why was he worrying about whether she liked his choice? It mattered because *she* mattered to him. In such a short time, Annie's kids had come to mean a lot to him. He didn't know he could feel this way. Swallowing hard, he picked up Spencer and put him on the sofa.

When Ian opened the book, Kara gazed up at him. "I like that one."

"Good." He looked over at Spencer. "You like this one, too?"

Spencer nodded, and Ian began the story about the princess and the frog. After he'd read the books in Kara's stack, he stood up. "That's it for story time tonight. The next on your mom's agenda is brushing your teeth. So off to the bathroom."

"Ah, do we have to?" Kara wrinkled her nose. "Mommy sometimes lets us watch a show."

"That was not on your mom's list."

Kara scooted off the sofa and went to the TV stand and pulled a video off the shelf. "See. Here's a good one."

Ian examined the case. Doreen Montgomery was written across the top. So his mom had given Annie some movies the granddaughters had outgrown. It was one of those fairy tales like the books he'd read tonight with the happy endings. He put the video back on the shelf. "It may be good, but you won't be watching it. It's time to brush your teeth."

Kara pouted, but she headed toward the bathroom with Spencer following. Grateful for her cooperation, Ian didn't know what he would've done if she'd refused. After they'd brushed their teeth and said their prayers, Ian tucked them into bed. As he pulled the covers under Kara's little chin, she gazed up at him. "If you marry our mom, you can be our daddy. I'd like that. Then we can live happily ever after. I think she likes you a lot. Can you marry her?"

There it was again. A little girl's wish. Last time Annie had rescued him from Kara's question. That wasn't going to happen tonight. He had to come up with some kind of answer.

"Only if she asks me." How would Kara respond?

Kara smiled. "I'll tell her to ask you."

Turning off the light, Ian wondered if Kara would actually do that, and what would Annie say about it? "Good night, kids."

"Good night," the tiny voices chorused.

With Kara's words floating through his mind, Ian went back into the living room and plopped down on the sofa. The little girl had been watching too many princess movies where they always lived happily ever after. Did that happen in real life? His parents had been married for over thirty-five years. His brothers' marriages were going strong after ten years. They all seemed happy. Guess he was the black sheep of the family, but then he'd always known that.

"Mr. Ian?"

Ian looked up to find Kara standing at the edge of the living room. "I forgot to tell you thank you for reading to me."

"You're welcome, Kara. Now back to bed."

The child turned and traipsed back down the hall. Ian suspected that he would see her a few more times before she finally went to sleep. He hoped she didn't disturb Spencer.

Sure enough. A couple minutes later, Kara reappeared. "I forgot to put my books away."

"That's okay. You might wake up Spencer if you put them away now."

"But Mommy says I should always put my things away."

Ian nodded. "That's a good rule, but I'll explain to her when she gets home."

"Okay." Kara slowly retraced her steps to the bedroom.

Ian hoped Kara was asleep by the time Annie returned. He didn't want her to think he was a terrible babysitter. The book he'd brought to read after the kids went to bed lay on the coffee table beside the children's books, but he wasn't sure he could concentrate enough to read it. His thoughts were filled with the laughter of two little kids and the pretty face of their mother. *Lord, what do You want me to do about Annie?*

Kara interrupted Ian's prayer. "I need a drink."

"Okay." Ian went into the kitchen with Kara and gave her a glass of water. When the child had finished drinking, he set the glass on the counter and looked at her. "Do you want me to get into trouble with your mom?" Kara shook her head. Ian hunkered down to her level. "Then you're going to have to go to bed and stay there. Can you do that?"

Kara nodded as Ian accompanied her down the hall and stood in the doorway while she got into bed. As he returned to the living room, he hoped his request would work to keep her in bed. Sitting on the sofa, he picked up his book again and opened it. He'd gone through a whole page before he realized he couldn't remember a thing he'd read.

Before he could start the page over, he heard a key in the door. Ian closed the book and stood as Annie walked in. A slow cooker in her arms, she went straight to the kitchen. She set it on the counter and turned to look at him. "Will you stay while I bring more stuff in?"

"Sure." He didn't have a chance to say another thing as she rushed out the door.

She returned carrying two plastic grocery bags loaded with something that smelled delicious.

"Do you need help?" He joined her in the kitchen.

She shook her head. "Got it under control. Your mother is an amazing cook. I hope I can cook half as well as she does when I'm finished with these lessons."

"I'm glad everything went well."

"I have meals for the rest of the week. No rushing home from work and trying to figure out what to fix for dinner." Annie put several freezer bags filled with food into the freezer, then turned to him. "How were the kids?"

"Good. We read lots of books." He pointed to

the books on the table. "Kara was worried you'd be upset that she didn't put them away. One of her many excuses for getting out of bed."

Annie laughed. "I should've warned you about that."

"I was prepared. My brothers told me that happened with their kids." Ian stood there trying to figure out what he should do. She was talking to him as if nothing had happened between them the last time he babysat. She'd wanted to talk about it then. Would she want to discuss it now? He took a deep breath. "Can we talk?"

"About what?"

"About the way I left the last time I was here."

"Sure." She tilted her head up to look at him. "What do you have to say?"

"I shouldn't have run off. I didn't know how to deal with what happened. I still don't." He was making a mess of this. Why hadn't he thought through what he was going to say? Did he dare tell her the incident had scared him? That probably wouldn't come across well. She wasn't going easy on him, either. She just stared at him. "What do you think?"

"Do you really want to know?"

"Yeah, or I wouldn't have asked."

Annie pointed at him then back at herself and then at him again. "Even after all this time and all the bad stuff, there's still something between us."

Ian swallowed hard. She didn't fear speaking the truth. "What do you want to do about it?"

"What do you want to do about it?" She was throwing the decision back on him.

Why not? He was the one who had brought it up again, and he was the one who had started everything with that kiss. Kara's wish floated through his mind. *If you marry our mom, you can be our daddy. I'd like that.* Was that why he'd brought up what happened the other night? "I wish I knew it could be a good thing."

"There's only one way to find out." Annie's gaze didn't waver as she stared at him. "We have to work on the relationship—get to really know one another again."

"We have to build the relationship on the right kinds of things this time."

"And you're willing to do that?" Incredulity etched itself across Annie's features.

Is that what he wanted? "Yes."

"Even with all my baggage and kids that belong to another man?"

"I love your kids." *And you, too.* He wasn't ready to tell Annie that even though it was evident he still did.

"Then how do we go about this?"

"We've already started—dominoes, bridge, visiting churches, even working on the finances together. But maybe we should go on a real date—just the two of us."

Annie smiled. "I'd like that."

"I'm pretty sure my parents will babysit. They're pushing for our reconciliation."

Annie grimaced. "Is that a good idea? If things don't work out, won't they be disappointed? I'd rather we keep this to ourselves."

"You might be right. I'll leave the babysitter up to you." So Annie wasn't sure about her feelings—the same as he was. They had to figure this out together. One day at a time. That's how he had to view this attempt to rebuild their relationship. She was willing to go out on a date. That had to be enough for now.

"I can trade with one of my neighbors."

"Okay." Ian tried not to let Annie's cautious view of their plans change his perspective. "When do you want to go on this date?"

"I'll let you know what day works for getting a babysitter."

"What would you like to do?"

Annie gave him an impish smile. "Surprise me."

"I can do that." Ian walked to the door. "Let me know about the day."

Annie nodded. "I'll call as soon as I find out."

Ian grabbed hold of the doorknob to keep himself from kissing Annie. That could wait until their date. "Good night."

As he drove home, he replayed their discussion in his mind. Did he want to marry Annie again? Put his heart on the line? Take responsibility for her children? Part of him wanted that very thing, but part of him worried that their reunion was unwise—a recipe for ruin again. But wouldn't they have God in the mix this time? That was a recipe for something good. He could only hope.

Chapter Twelve

The following Friday afternoon, Annie studied the monthly financial report and compared it with the report from the same month in the previous year. Expenses were down. The whole financial situation looked better at The Village, but the red ink still hadn't disappeared. Melody was preparing the latest newsletter while Adam made phone calls to churches to set up more mission talks.

Ian sat nearby, his head down, as he put together the report for the board of directors. She forced herself not to look his way. If she did, her mind would take her on a wishful journey of love, marriage and happily ever after.

For the past week, she'd tried to keep everything low-key with Ian, but their date tomorrow night was never far from her mind. Putting too much stock in their date could lead to disappointment. She didn't want to build up her hopes. In recent weeks, Ian had spent most of his days in court or working with clients and their cases, so he wasn't around much while Annie was working on the finances. Even their interaction today had been minimal as they worked on their own projects.

Annie hadn't said anything to anyone about their date. Even when she'd asked her neighbor to baby-sit, she only said she was going out. Fear that the budding reconciliation would fail kept her from mentioning it to anyone. She didn't know whether Ian had told anyone. She guessed he hadn't because the subject never came up in conversation.

When five o'clock arrived, Annie shut down her workstation and gathered her belongings. She went over to Ian and waved to Melody, who was leaving.

He glanced up and smiled as she approached. "Good news?"

"Not bad, but I have so many ideas that we still need to put in place. Do you think the board will see the progress and give us more time?"

Ian leaned over and pulled up a chair beside him. "Do you have a minute to talk?"

Annie glanced at the clock. "A few. I have to pick up the kids. The day care workers don't mind going a little over, but not too much."

"Okay. I'll make it quick." Ian pointed to the file he had up on his computer screen. "See what I'm showing?"

Annie studied the graphs. The upward trend lines

made her smile. "That's what I've got in mine, too. I sent you the file before I shut down the computer. Did you get it?"

Ian found the file Annie had sent him and opened it. "This is all good. I'm not sure we can persuade Bob Franklin with this report, but I believe it will be enough to show the majority of the board that we're on the right track. Thanks for doing such a good job."

Ian's praise made Annie's heart skitter. "I hope I get to do a lot more."

"Everything still good for tomorrow?"

Smiling, Annie nodded. "We're all set."

"I'll talk to you later. I'm going to stay and work some more."

"Okay." Annie rushed away.

When she was halfway across the quad, she realized in her hurry she had left her bag by Ian's computer station. She raced back to the administration building. As she approached the office door, she heard Ian say her name. Why was he talking about her?

"What will happen when she finds out? Should I tell her and hope for the best?" Ian's question made Annie's heart jump into her throat as she hesitated in the hallway. What was he talking about?

"Pray about it." Adam's answer floated into the hallway. "But my first instinct is that you should tell her before she finds out from someone else you were the one to report her to DFCS."

Annie stifled a gasp. Why had he done this to her? A light-headed sensation coming over her, she leaned against the wall. No wonder he hadn't wanted to represent her. With all kinds of thoughts whirling in her mind, she couldn't think straight. Should she get her bag and confront him? Maybe it would be better that way.

Ian had been all rah, rah, rah about how well she was doing—how happy he was that she and her kids were together and that they should see whether they could repair their broken relationship, but he hadn't been honest with her. The betrayal stung.

Her heart thudding, Annie took a deep breath and marched into the office. "You don't have to worry about telling me. I heard everything."

Holding up his hands, Adam backed away. "I'll leave you two alone."

Ian stepped closer. "I'm sorry you had to find out that way."

"I'm sure you are." Dodging Ian's attempt to reach out to her, Annie picked up her bag and held it as if it could shield her from the hurt. "Why?"

"You took money from me and used it to buy drugs rather than food for your kids. You stole from me." Ian crossed his arms at his waist. "I did it for the kids, but I admit my anger played a part. I won't sugarcoat it. I wanted you to hurt as much as I hurt."

Annie glared at him. "Well, you got your wish. I hurt plenty. I missed a whole year of my kids' lives. Are you happy about that?"

"No. I'm sad that it had to be."

"Well, you don't have to worry about any date tomorrow or any other time." Annie turned and raced from the room.

"Annie, wait."

Annie didn't stop. She raced across the quad. She didn't want to listen to Ian's apologies or excuses or judgments. She wanted to hug her kids and pretend that Ian Montgomery didn't exist.

After dropping off her kids at day care, Annie traipsed across the quad to go to work on the finances. The days since she'd learned of Ian's part in having her children taken away had held unhappiness and doubts. Her depressing mood had even triggered passing thoughts of getting high—just so she could have that sense of euphoria again. But the sweet faces of her children saved her every time.

Besides, if she gave in to the temptation, she would prove Ian right—that she couldn't stay clean and sober. She would stay strong. She would win— one day at a time. She let the mantra roll through her mind.

As she entered the administration building,

Melody stepped out of her office. "Annie, just the person I want to see."

"About what?"

"Come in and we'll talk."

"Sure." Annie didn't have a good feeling as she followed Melody and sat in the chair next to her desk.

Melody eyed Annie. "What's the trouble between you and Ian?"

"Besides that fact we're divorced?"

"Old news." Melody shook her head. "I'm talking about your request not to visit churches with him and the way you two are avoiding each other. You were getting along so well, and suddenly you're not. I'm concerned."

Annie wondered what to say. Should she tell Melody what Ian had done? Should she mention the encounter with Jesse? Annie didn't want to talk about any of it. "Thanks for your concern, but this is something Ian and I have to work out on our own."

Melody leaned forward. "I suppose you think I'm butting in where I don't belong, but I see how sad this has made you. I wanted to be sure your sobriety wasn't in jeopardy."

Annie shouldn't be afraid to talk to Melody, but she couldn't bring herself to open up. "I'll remember that."

"Good." Melody sighed. "Just one more thing. I

believe Ian still loves you *and* your kids. He's never found someone else. You and Ian belong together."

Annie twisted her hands in her lap as she struggled to believe Melody's statement. It was wishful thinking. She'd alienated Ian again with her unforgiving words, and although the separation from her children for a year lay squarely on her, Ian's part in it hurt—hurt deeply. "I don't see that happening."

"Pray about it. I will." Melody touched Annie's arm. "Would you like to do that now?"

Annie nodded, not trusting herself to speak. She prayed silently along with Melody as she asked for wisdom and strength for Annie. The prayer brought peace to Annie's heart.

When Melody's prayer ended, Annie looked up. "Thanks."

"Anytime. I'm here to help. Just ask."

"There's one favor I'd like to ask of you."

Melody nodded. "Anything."

"It's been several weeks since my failed attempt to talk to my parents. During that meeting my mom never said anything while my dad bellowed at me." Annie shrugged. "I got the feeling my mom wanted to talk to me. I thought I could see it in her eyes, but I wasn't sure."

"So what are you saying?" Melody knit her eyebrows.

"I haven't been able to get her expression out of my mind. Then today Kara brought home a notice about grandparent's day at day care in a couple of weeks. She wanted to know why she didn't have grandparents." Annie swallowed hard. "It broke my heart. I think I should try to talk to my mother— alone."

"What do you plan to do?"

"My mom often works at home. I thought I'd try to see her tomorrow after work because if everything remains as it was, my dad has his regular guy's night out. Without him there maybe she'd give me a chance to show her these." Annie reached for her purse and extracted an envelope. "Doreen gave me the photos she took on Mother's Day."

Melody shuffled through them, then looked up at Annie. "What grandmother could resist these children?"

Annie smiled, her eyes a little misty. "That's what I thought, too."

"So what's the favor?"

"Could you pick up the kids from day care and watch them until I get home?"

"Absolutely." Melody hugged Annie. "I'll be praying for you the whole time."

The sun sat just above the tree line in the western sky and made for difficult driving as Annie went to her parents' house. Even the visor in Cora's old car didn't help to obscure the sun's brightness. Tension eased from Annie's shoulders as she turned into the neighborhood where her parents lived. She gripped the steering wheel and said a prayer as she parked in front of her parents' house.

She sat in the car for a few moments and gathered her thoughts. She reviewed what she planned to say when her mother answered the door. Could she get her mother to let her inside again? Annie said a prayer as she got out of the vehicle.

As she shut the door, a hand clamped over her mouth, an arm went around her upper chest and something hard pressed against her back. A streak of fear shivered down her spine. Her heart thundered in her ears. She froze.

"That's right. Don't move. Don't make a sound, and everything'll be okay." Jesse's harsh voice sounded in her ear.

The smell of alcohol and the stench of his unbathed body nearly gagged her, but she forced the reflex back. She'd been so focused on what she was going to do and say that she hadn't seen him. But she would never have thought to check her surroundings in her parents' quiet neighborhood. And how would Jesse know she would be there?

"I've got a gun and if you want to see your kids again, you do exactly as I say." Jesse slid the gun down her back until it rested just below her rib cage. "Now we're going to walk nice and slow up to the door. You may not have any money, but your parents are loaded."

Annie let him lead her up the front walk and onto the porch. She had brought trouble to her parents' door. Now they would never forgive her.

With the gun still pointed at her, Jesse stepped aside so anyone answering the door wouldn't see him. "Do what I say, and I won't hurt you."

Annie nodded, her legs trembling.

"Ring the bell, and don't say a thing." Jesse motioned with the gun.

Hoping that her mother wasn't home, Annie pressed the bell. The chime sounded through the door and a moment later her mother appeared.

Before Annie could do anything, Jesse grabbed her and pushed her inside. Her mother screamed as Jesse waved the gun at both of them. "Shut up, get in the living room and sit on the couch."

Annie held back her tears as she looked at her mom. "I'm so sorry."

"Zip it, you…"

Annie cringed at Jesse's expletives and grabbed her mom's hand. She squeezed it tight. Annie couldn't think straight. Her wonderful plan was in ruins. Would Jesse let them go when he got what he wanted, or would he shoot them with that gun? Annie wanted to believe he wasn't capable of such a thing, but he was high on something. There was no telling what he might do.

He pulled a rope out of his pocket and tossed it at Annie. "Tie your mother's hands behind her back."

Annie did as Jesse instructed and hoped following his directions would win them a reprieve. After she'd tied her mother's hands, he waved the gun for her to sit down. He pulled out another piece of rope, but before he could tie Annie's hands, her father came in the front door. Jesse turned and fired the gun. The bullet slammed into the door frame. Her father ducked. Annie and her mother screamed.

"Down on the floor." Jesse waved the gun wildly.

Annie went facedown on the floor and her father did the same while her mother sat ashen faced on the couch. As Annie lay there, she remembered the cell phone in her pocket. If she could hit the right button, she could call someone on speed dial. Maybe they would be able to tell she was in trouble. While Jesse tied up her father with the rope he'd first intended for her, Annie surreptitiously felt for her phone. She flipped it open, punched a button and prayed that Jesse wouldn't discover it before someone on the other end figured out what was happening.

The sounds of jovial conversation and the clatter of dishes greeted Ian as he surveyed the restaurant. He spied his dad joking with one of the waitresses as she placed two menus on the table. He and his dad hadn't met for their usual Friday lunch in nearly six weeks. Even this meeting they'd postponed until after work. The last time they'd met was right before Mother's Day.

Ian slipped into the booth. "Finally made it. Sorry I was late. I've been working on my part of the financial report for the board."

"Glad you could make it tonight since your mother has that ladies' program." His dad glanced at the menu, then put it aside. "How's your finance thing going?"

"The report is nearly done, but I'm not sure it'll satisfy the board. The financial situation is much better, but I don't see us being in the black until the end of the year after some of our adjustments are in place for a few months."

"Won't the board realize that when you present the report?"

Ian shrugged. "I would hope so, but Bob Franklin is a stickler for results—results he can see now."

"Maybe we need to pray that the Lord will soften Bob's heart and give him a vision for the future of this ministry."

"I wish I had your faith, Dad." Ian sighed.

"And I wish I had your heart for the underprivileged. You've helped me realize that even if only one person has a closer walk with God then it's worth every penny spent on that transformation. People are more important than money. I know the Lord has worked on my heart. The change I've seen in Annie has convinced me your ministry is one that needs to continue."

Ian nodded, not wanting to talk about Annie. He feared his dad would bring up the question he'd tried to ask during Annie's testimony at church.

"What's going on with you and Annie?"

Ian wasn't sure he knew how to answer that question. He let out a harsh breath. "She found out I was the one who turned her in to DFCS."

"I didn't know that."

"I never told anyone, except the person at DFCS, but I was afraid for those children."

Jordan nodded. "You don't have to defend your actions."

"I wish Annie felt that way."

The waitress returned to take their order and gave Ian a respite from his dad's inquisition. After she left, his dad gave him a speculative look. "It's no secret your mother and I think it would be wonderful if you two got back together."

"I don't see that happening now." Ian frowned. "Besides, maybe it's for the best. What good would come from reuniting two recovering substance abusers?"

"You're different people now. You have God in your lives."

"Annie has made it pretty clear she's not interested in getting back together."

Jordan paused to say a prayer after the waitress

delivered their food. After the prayer, he looked up. "Aren't you two visiting churches together?"

"We were until Annie found out what I did. She felt betrayed and used the difficulty of finding a sitter as an excuse not to go." Ian took a bite of his burger and chewed slowly. He hoped his dad would eat and not badger him further.

Jordan took a gulp of his iced tea, then set the glass down. "I get the impression you don't want to talk about Annie."

"You would be correct." Ian laughed halfheartedly. Couldn't his dad drop this conversation?

"I wish I could fix this for you. I think you and Annie belong together."

"She doesn't."

"Have you told her you still love her?"

"She doesn't want to talk to me." Ian stared at his half-eaten burger. He'd been telling himself for weeks that he was falling in love again, but in truth he'd never stopped loving Annie. His love had been buried under a mountain of hurt, anger and unforgiveness. Little by little Annie and her changed life had chipped away at that mountain until those feelings were unearthed.

Jordan wagged a finger at Ian. "If you love her, you have to find a way to tell her."

Was his dad right? Ian could hear Kara's little voice echoing in his brain. *I think she likes you a lot.* Was that still true? If he wanted to know, he had to be willing to put his heart on the line. "I wish I knew how."

"Would you like your mother to invite Annie and the kids over to eat? Your mother is itching to have some time with Kara and Spencer."

Ian shook his head. "I'm not sure she would come. I need to handle this on my own."

"Don't wait too long."

Before Ian could respond, his cell phone buzzed in his pocket. He pulled it out. Annie's name appeared on the display. Why was she calling? He looked at his dad. "It's Annie."

"Answer it." His dad grinned.

Ian put the phone to his ear. "Hi, Annie." There was no response. "Hello." Garbled conversation came through the phone. He couldn't make out anything. "Hello?"

His dad leaned forward. "Bad connection?"

Ian held the phone out and stared at it. When he was about to end the connection and call back, a scream sounded over the phone. He looked at his dad. "What's going on?"

Concern colored his dad's expression. "Listen for a moment."

Ian turned up the volume and laid the phone on the table, not caring whether he was disturbing those around them. More garbled voices came over the phone. Then he heard Annie. "Jesse, if you kill my parents, you won't get any money."

Ian's heart jumped into his throat as he picked up the phone, put it on mute and scrambled out of the booth. "Annie's in trouble. It sounds like her old boyfriend is holding her hostage. I've got to help her."

His dad put a hand on Ian's arm. "Wait a minute, son. Calm down. We have to figure out where she is."

Ian took a deep breath, his heart still pounding as he listened to the muffled conversation coming over the phone's speaker. His dad was right. "Call Melody and see if she knows anything."

After his dad talked to Melody and discovered Annie's whereabouts, Ian still monitored his phone as he started for the door. If he could only tell what was happening. Was Annie still okay? *Please, God, keep her safe.* The prayer flitted through his mind as he looked at his dad. "Call 911. I'm heading over there."

Jordan raced after Ian as he made the call. "Let the police take care of this. You can't do anything."

Still listening to his phone, Ian paced back and forth next to his car as his dad explained the situation to the 911 operator. He looked up at Ian. "Do you know the address?"

Ian rattled off the address, thankful that he still remembered it. "I'm going over there."

Jordan ended the call. "The police are on their

way. I don't think you should go, but if you're going, I'm going, too."

Ian opened the door to his car. "Get in, because you can't stop me."

Chapter Thirteen

Her heart beating in overtime, Annie lay perfectly still on the floor while Jesse roamed around the room. He waved the gun in the air and hurled profanity-laced insults at her and her parents. Annie didn't dare look at her father, who lay tied up beside her, for fear Jesse would think she was up to something and discover her phone. She forced herself not to cry as she closed her eyes and prayed for God to send someone to save them.

Jesse continued to pace back and forth as he shouted about the unfairness of life. Annie remembered having that paranoid feeling when drugs had controlled her thoughts. Everything and everyone had been against her. Thank the Lord for saving her from that miserable life. Surely, God hadn't brought her this far to wind up dead at the hands of her drunken ex-boyfriend. Kara and Spencer needed her.

With the rug chafing her cheek, Annie thought about Ian and the way she had sent him away with angry words. He'd done the right thing when he had reported her to DFCS. She'd been an unfit mother, and he was only protecting her children. She'd let the shock of learning he was responsible for the loss of her children make her say things she shouldn't have said. Would she live to tell him she'd been wrong—to ask for his forgiveness again?

Shivers ran down Annie's spine as Jesse pressed the gun to her cheek. She held her breath and prayed. What was he going to do?

"Do what I say, and no one gets hurt." Jesse yanked on Annie's arm and pulled her to her feet.

With the gun's cold metal against her skin, Annie didn't dare breathe. Jesse shoved her onto the couch next to her mother, who was sobbing.

"Shut up. Quit crying, or I'll shoot." Jesse waved his gun under her mother's nose. Then Jesse stood over her father. "I want you to get me one hundred thousand dollars and safe passage to Croatia."

Her father turned his head up to look at Jesse. "I can't do anything while I'm tied up on the floor."

Jesse blinked as if he was trying to make a judgment about her father's statement. Jesse wasn't rational if he thought he could get those things. Afraid to look at her mother, Annie tried to remain calm. She glanced out the window to see whether anyone might have called the police. Nothing. No one knew they were trapped in this house with a madman. Annie closed her eyes and prayed.

Jesse poked the gun against her temple. "Why are you closing your eyes?"

Annie wondered what Jesse would say if she told him she was praying for him. Would he listen to her if she tried to persuade him to stop this madness?

Before Annie could answer, sirens sounded in the distance. Jesse turned toward the window as the sirens' wail grew louder. Annie looked outside. Flashing red-and-blue lights accompanied the screaming sirens. Jesse pointed the gun at Annie. Her heart jumped into her throat.

Jesse's face twisted with rage. "Who called the police?"

Taking a deep breath, Annie hoped her expression didn't give anything away. "One of the neighbors must have heard the gunshot."

Jesse narrowed his gaze as he glanced between her and the commotion outside. Then he sneered. "Maybe it's a good thing the police showed up. Now I'll get some action."

A voice boomed over a police megaphone. "This is Sergeant Brad McGarvey, Police Department Crisis Unit. I'm here to listen to you and to try to make sure everybody stays safe."

Annie held her breath and waited to see what Jesse would do. Eventually, the officer established a phone connection with Jesse, and Annie had hopes the police could talk sense into him. But the conversation went on and on, and she couldn't tell what was going on from listening to only one side of the conversation.

Despite Jesse's bravado about getting action out of the police, he disconnected the call and stood against the wall between two windows and waved his gun at Annie and her parents. "They're just stalling. No action from anyone."

Annie stared at Jesse. That's who she had been until a street preacher had taken the time to show her God's mercy and point her in the right direction. She had to try to do that for Jesse now rather than dismiss him as a lost cause as some had done with her, including her parents and Ian. *Lord, give me the right words to say.*

"Jesse—"

"Shut up." He waved the gun at her and her mother stifled a sob.

"Please listen to me. I want to help you."

Jesse's lips twisted in a snarl and he laughed. "What? Now you're going to give me money."

"No. I told you before I don't have any money, but I've got something better."

"Like what?"

"God's love."

"Don't preach at me."

"I'm not going to preach. I'm just going to tell you what God did for me." Annie nodded. "He forgave me and gave me a new life, and it's wonderful. I'm not craving the next drink or the next hit. My mind is clear. You can have God's love, too. He doesn't care what you've done. He's ready to give you a new and better life."

"Yeah, yeah, yeah. You've turned into a do-gooder just like that ex-husband of yours. Tell me another good story."

"Jesse, whether you believe me or not, what good is it going to do you to harm us? The police have the place surrounded. You can't escape no matter what you do to us." Annie wondered whether any of her statements soaked into his fuzzy mind. "At least let my mother go. You still have me and my dad, who has the money."

Jesse eyed her as if he wasn't sure whether he could believe her. "So if I let your mother go, I'll get the money?"

Annie was pretty sure she shouldn't make any blanket promises. What answer would satisfy Jesse? "I think that would help. Please release her."

During the drive, Ian listened to his phone. He could barely tell what anyone was saying unless someone shouted. Things had been very quiet, and Ian worried that Annie was hurt. When he arrived, a couple of squad cars and a SWAT team were there. He parked his car down the street and walked toward the officer setting up a barricade. Jordan followed close behind. Even from a distance, Ian could tell that an officer was in communication with someone in the house. Ian swallowed the lump in his throat as he drew near to the barricade.

The officer looked up at Ian. "You can't come any farther."

Ian held up his phone. "One of the hostages called me, and the call is still connected. I believe the gunman knows nothing about it."

After Ian explained his and his dad's relationship to Annie, the officer indicated that they should come with him. They were fitted with vests before they related their story to the lead hostage negotiator, who thanked them for the new information and told them about Jesse's demands.

Would Jesse leave his hostages unharmed if he received those things? Annie's parents were wealthy enough to give him what he wanted, but how would they react? Would they blame Annie for bringing this trouble on them? Ian couldn't imagine what Annie must be going through. He wanted to rush into the house and save her. A foolish notion, for sure. He felt totally helpless.

While Ian paced and continued to monitor his phone at the police officer's request, Jordan stepped into Ian's path. "Pacing isn't going to help anything. Let's take a moment to pray."

"Okay." Ian stopped and bowed his head and listened to his dad's prayer. Ian remembered how his dad's prayers had brought him through the pain of his accident and withdrawal from the drugs and alcohol. How had he ever doubted that his dad cared about him? Annie's reemergence in their lives had brought his dad and him closer. They understood each other better now than ever. Ian tried to reassure himself that they would get through this crisis with God's help.

As Jordan ended his prayer, a commotion broke out near the house. Ian jerked his head toward the sound. Annie's mother stepped out the front door. She sobbed as an officer rushed to greet her. Ian couldn't tell what she was saying. He had to find out if Annie was okay. He moved closer. Annie's mother tried to talk in between sobs, but she was nearly hysterical.

Jordan approached one of the officers. "Sir, I was Mrs. Payton's pastor for a number of years. May I talk with her and see if I can calm her?"

The officer nodded, leading them to a safe area away from the house. Ian followed his father as he went to talk to Marcia. When she saw Ian, she covered her face with her hands. Jordan put his arm around her shoulders. "It's okay, Marcia. You're safe. Let's pray for Annie and Richard."

Nodding, Marcia let out another little sob as she bowed her head. After Jordan finished, Marcia appeared to have regained some of her composure, and she recounted what had happened. Ian thanked

God that no one had been hurt when Jesse fired the gun, but the knowledge that the man had shot at Richard made Ian's stomach sink. They had to get Annie and her dad out of there.

Misery painted every inch of Marcia's face. "I was reluctant to leave, but Annie and Richard insisted. If only I had talked to her when she came the first time, this wouldn't have happened. Annie was so brave when she talked that horrible man into letting me go."

At least Marcia had said something positive about Annie. How would this affect Annie's relationship with her parents?

Ian pointed to his phone. "Annie called me. So we've been listening to what's happening although we can't make out most of it. The police said to let them know if we hear anything new."

"Did you hear the gunshot?" Marcia asked.

Ian shook his head. "She must've called after that happened. When we realized what was going on, we called 911."

"Thank you." Marcia put a hand over her heart. "I never saw Annie with a phone."

"She must have it hidden. That's probably why we can't hear very well."

Marcia leaned closer "So you can't tell what's happening?"

"Not most of the time. The voices are muffled. We heard the shouting."

"It was awful. I was so frightened." Marcia put a hand to her mouth.

Jordan waved his hand in a circle. "It looks like the SWAT team has the house surrounded."

Marcia wrung her hands. "They're supposed to know what they're doing, but that guy is crazy—hopped up on some kind of drugs."

Ian wondered what Marcia thought about his presence there. Did she find it strange? She hadn't indicated any surprise. He wasn't sure what to say to his ex-mother-in-law. They'd never been close even when he'd been married to Annie. He was pretty sure they blamed him for Annie's downfall.

The time dragged as Ian waited for news. The phone connection became more and more garbled until Ian considered ending the call, but he feared losing that link to Annie. He wanted to be there if he could somehow help her. Why weren't the police making more progress? How long could this go on? Soon it would be dark. Were the police waiting until darkness to make their move?

As the last rays of sunlight slithered through the tall pines, the SWAT team made a single-file line. Ian prayed like he'd never prayed before. Before the SWAT team made their first move, the front door opened slightly and a white flag waved through the opening. The officers held their ground as the door opened completely and a man stepped out with his hands raised in the air. The police immediately took him into custody. Moments later Annie and her father appeared on the front porch. Marcia ran to greet them. They hugged and cried and talked all at once. Ian wanted more than anything to be part of that reunion, but he didn't belong.

Ian turned to his dad. "Guess we ought to be going."

Jordan raised his eyebrows. "You're not going to talk to Annie?"

Ian motioned toward the Paytons, who were now talking with the police. "Does it look like I have any chance to talk to her?"

"You should at least let her know you're here."

Ian shook his head. "I can't intrude. I know she's safe. It looks like she's had reconciliation with her parents. That's good enough for right now."

Jordan shook his head. "I hope you know what you're doing."

"I do." Ian turned toward his car.

"Ian, wait." Annie's voice sounded over the commotion.

Ian turned as Annie ran toward him, her parents close behind.

"Are you okay?" The question sounded lame, but he had no idea what else to say.

Nodding, she stopped in front of him as she tried to catch her breath. "Thank you. Mom told me you're the one who alerted the police."

"Melody told us where you were."

Annie shook her head. "I had no idea who would get the call. I just happened to press the number that speed dials your phone."

"I'm glad I was there to help, and we can thank God for cell phones and speed dialing." Ian wished he could tell Annie everything he was thinking and feeling, but he couldn't do that with an audience. So instead, he shook hands with the Paytons as they expressed their gratitude. "Is there anything we can do for you? You want me to check on Kara and Spencer? You might be here for a while talking to the police."

Annie shook her head. "Melody is already with the kids. I'll talk to her."

"Okay. We'll talk later." Ian hoped so. Would today's events give him an opportunity to plead his case?

A lot of bad feelings had passed between the two families after Ian and Annie's divorce. At least the falling-out between Annie and her parents seemed to be on the mend. They stood there for a moment in awkward silence until an officer herded the Paytons away.

"That was a little tense." Ian glanced over at his dad as they made their way to the car.

Jordan nodded. "I don't know that any of us knew what to say, but I have a feeling Annie wanted to say more than she did."

"Yeah, I got that feeling, too, but we need some privacy to sort things out."

"I agree, but don't put it off."

After Ian dropped off his dad, he thought about their conversation. Ian wished he could have talked with Annie right then because he feared time and distance would weaken his resolve to tell her how he felt. The way they had parted after their last meeting left the possibility of rejection and another broken heart. He had to start being the kind of man who went after what he wanted. And he wanted Annie's love.

Chapter Fourteen

Annie's apartment gleamed. Kara and Spencer were dressed in their new outfits. Thanks to Doreen's excellent cooking lessons, Annie had dinner in the oven. She tried not to be nervous as she checked over each room one more time, then herded Kara and Spencer into the kitchen so she could make a last-minute check on the food. She wanted everything to be perfect for her parents' visit.

Kara tugged on Annie's arm as she checked the sauce simmering on the stove. "Mommy, are they going to be here soon?"

"Yes, sweetie. When this hand gets on the twelve." Annie pointed to the clock and tried not to let Kara's umpteenth inquiry annoy her. Five minutes was forever to a four-year-old.

"But it's taking so long." Kara wrinkled her nose. "Is Mr. Ian coming, too?"

Annie shook her head. "Just your grandma and grandpa tonight."

"I miss Mr. Ian. I like when he reads stories to us." Head tilted, Kara stared at Annie. "Mr. Ian says he'll marry you and be our daddy if you ask him."

Kara's statement nearly made Annie drop the spoon in the sauce. Had Ian really said that, or was Kara making stuff up because that's what she wanted?

The intercom buzzer sounded. Her parents were here. Annie didn't have time to think about Kara's pronouncement. She grabbed the tray of appetizers, plates and napkins and deposited it on the coffee table on her way to the intercom. She buzzed her mother and father into the building and opened the door of her apartment as they walked down the hallway. Her mind whirled with Kara's declaration and her parents' arrival. Annie took a calming breath. She would deal with her parents tonight and Ian tomorrow.

Annie hugged her mother and father, then held her breath as they stepped inside. Kara and Spencer stood near the doorway and stared up at their grandparents.

Annie slowly released her breath as her dad hunkered down next to Spencer. "You must be Spencer. I'm your grandpa Richard."

Spencer shied away, hiding behind one of Annie's legs.

Kara stepped forward and puffed out her chest.

"Hi, Grandpa Richard. I'm Kara. Spencer's shy cuz he's little. I'm big."

"You can call me Grandma Marcia. We brought you something." Marcia handed a small gift bag to each of the children."

The children tore into the tissue paper in the bags. Kara found a fashion doll in her bag, and Spencer discovered a toy truck. Annie instructed the children to say thank you, then wondered what to do next.

"Something smells really good." Marcia glanced toward the kitchen.

Annie turned in a panic. "Yeah, I'd better check to make sure nothing's burning. Help yourself to the appetizers."

"We will while your father and I get to know the children better," her mother called as Annie fled to the kitchen.

When Annie returned, her parents were actually playing with Kara and Spencer. Annie stood there and watched. She never remembered her parents doing anything like that when she was a kid. They'd always been too busy. Perhaps being grandparents would change them.

"Everything's ready." Annie motioned toward the table she had set with elaborate care.

Marcia looked Annie's way. "Anything I can do to help?"

"Just help the kids into their booster seats." Annie

brought the main dish to the table and quickly followed with the side dishes.

With everyone seated, she said a short prayer, then passed the chicken dish to her father. Silence enveloped the room as everyone started eating. Annie nibbled on her own food, hardly able to enjoy it as she waited to see what her parents thought.

Her father looked up and smiled. "This is very good."

Annie let herself smile as she drank in the compliment. "It's Doreen Montgomery's recipe. She's been helping me learn to cook."

"How wonderful. I remember her being an excellent cook. I'm glad you've had a good teacher." Marcia shook her head and smiled. "I didn't help you much on that account."

"I didn't care about learning to cook when I lived at home. I probably wouldn't have been much of a student."

"You wouldn't want cooking lessons from your mother, anyway." Richard chuckled.

Marcia frowned at her husband. "You aren't starving."

Winking, Richard patted Marcia's arm. "I know, dear. I was just kidding."

"Enough kidding." Marcia turned to Kara. "What's your favorite food?"

"Pizza."

"Just like your mother." Marcia laughed as she looked at Annie, then turned her attention to Spencer. "What do you like?"

Spencer scrunched up his little face. "Hot dogs. Do you like hot dogs?"

Richard gave a big belly laugh. "Spencer, your grandma does not like hot dogs, but I do. I'll have to take you to the Varsity someday for a hot dog."

"What's the Varsity?" Kara wrinkled her nose. "Do I get to come, too?"

"Sure, if you like hot dogs." Richard smiled at Kara. "The Varsity is a famous food joint in Atlanta, and they serve all kinds of hot dogs."

"I like them as much as Spencer." Kara wrinkled her nose and squinted her eyes as she looked at her grandparents. "How come I haven't seen you before?"

Annie held her breath. What would her parents say? How could they explain their absence from the lives of their grandchildren? She didn't want to say anything bad about her parents. Getting over old hurts was part of the forgiveness she had to work toward, but she should've known inquisitive Kara would ask such a question. Would any explanation suffice?

Marcia looked at Annie as if she were trying to get some guidance on how to answer. Then she turned her attention to the little girl. "Kara, we're so sorry we didn't get to know you sooner, but your mommy was very sick for a long time, and we didn't know how to help her. She is better now, and we will see you as often as we can."

Annie listened to her mother's statement. This was a two-way street. She couldn't blame the estrangement between her and her parents completely on them. She had let her own insecurities lead her toward a destructive life. Her brother had grown up in the same environment, but he hadn't let their parents' inattention cause him to make bad choices.

When the meal was over, Marcia helped Annie with the cleanup while her father played with the children. Afterward, her parents helped Annie put the children to bed. She could hardly believe what she was seeing when her mom and dad started to read a story to the children. Back in the living room with her parents, Annie wondered if they would stay longer, or were they eager to go home.

Marcia gestured around the room. "Annie, you've done a wonderful job decorating your apartment."

"Thanks." Annie smiled broadly, knowing this was high praise from her mother, the interior designer.

Richard nodded. "And you have two beautiful children who are so well-behaved."

Annie tried to smile. "I can't take all the credit for that. They had a wonderful foster family while I was in rehab."

Marcia came over and gave Annie a hug. "I'm so

glad you finally got help. We should've been there for you, and we weren't. We didn't know what to do, so we did nothing. Can you forgive us?"

Annie stepped back and stared at her mother. Forgiving and being forgiven. Annie's life was full of it. She had begged for Ian's forgiveness. Now her parents asked her for the same. She swallowed hard and nodded. "That's something I'm working on. I know I've done a lot to alienate you. I hope the future will be different."

"Thank you. I know that doesn't come easy. We've done some soul-searching in the last few days. A brush with death will do that to a person." Tears welling in her eyes, Marcia reached over and took Annie's hand.

"Is it okay if we sit down and talk for a few minutes?" Richard motioned toward the sofa.

"Sure." Annie took the chair while her parents sat together on the sofa. "What do you want to talk about?"

"There's a lot we have to say." Richard leaned forward. "First, I want to say I'm proud of you for making the needed changes in your life. I know it wasn't easy. Secondly, we've decided to rededicate our lives to God. You've shown us what that means in your life."

Marcia nodded. "Your testimony to Jesse about having Jesus in your life saved us in more ways than one. He didn't want to listen at first, but you kept talking in that quiet, composed voice. Your calmness showed him the peace you have in your life because of your faith. I saw the tension just drain out of him. He didn't want to fight a losing battle with you or the police. God touched his heart through you."

"He'll have to spend time in prison, but I hope he gets the help he needs. Pastor John from the rehab center is going to talk to Jesse." Annie grimaced. "I'm so sorry you had to go through that because of me. I should've told someone that Jesse had threatened me before. I had no idea he'd been stalking me just waiting for the chance to get to you and your money. I was afraid any association with him would jeopardize everything with Kara and Spencer." Annie pressed her lips together and hoped her parents would understand. "Now I know I was wrong."

"Right or wrong. We see that God used the situation to help us see our mistakes." Richard looked at his wife. "We want to make things right with you. We've also decided that we're going to make a very generous contribution to The Village of Hope. We see how much it has helped you."

"Thank you. Thank you. It will be a blessing to so many people here." Annie got up and hugged her parents. "You'll have to tell Ian so he can include it in the financial report he's giving to the board."

"I have a better idea." Marcia reached into her

purse. "We'll write the check now, and you can give it to Ian."

"Okay." Annie wondered what her parents thought about Ian. Did she dare ask?

"Here." Marcia held out the check.

When Annie took it, she marveled at her parents' generosity. "Mom, Dad, this is way more than I ever expected. This will do so much good here."

Her mother gave her a hug. "We love you."

Then her dad hugged her. "You can thank us by staying away from drugs and alcohol and letting us see our darling grandchildren often."

"With God's help, I will. I love you, too." They joined in a group hug.

Her dad stepped back. "Now I want to know what is happening between you and Ian."

Annie's mind spun. She didn't know the answer. "We've resolved a lot of animosity between us."

"Does that mean you might reconcile?" Marcia asked.

Annie shook her head, then recounted Ian's and her journey to forgiving each other. "What do you think about it?"

Marcia gave Annie's shoulders a squeeze. "It doesn't matter what we think. We want you to be happy. I believe God will help you decide what is best for both of you. I know He has shown us our need to change our lives."

Annie nodded. "Pray for me."

"And you for us." Richard kissed the top of Annie's head. "We've got to get going. Thanks for the wonderful food and time with our grandchildren. Make plans to come over to the house after church on Sunday."

"I will." Annie stood in the doorway and waved as her parents left.

After she closed the door, she wanted to scream with delight, but she didn't want to wake the children. Instead, she high stepped around the apartment and finished with a victorious pose, her hands raised above her head. She couldn't quit smiling. Annie wanted to tell Ian about the donation at this very moment, but she would wait until tomorrow. She would give him the donation, and then she would propose. If Kara was right, he would say yes.

Picking up his buzzing cell phone from his desk, Ian saw that Annie was calling. His heart raced as he answered. "Hi, Annie. I'm sorry I haven't talked to you before now, but—"

"I don't need any excuses or apologies. I want to talk to you tonight after work. Where can we meet?"

"Would you like to go out to eat?"

"No, this is business." Her no-nonsense tone told him this wasn't a social call.

"You know people do conduct business over a meal."

"I'd rather not discuss the finances of The Village in a public place."

"Okay, I see. How about pizza in my office? Our usual?"

"That works for me. I'll see you around five-thirty."

After the call ended, Ian stared at his phone. He hadn't asked her why she wanted to discuss the finances at this late date. Her phone call had him completely discombobulated. But today he was going to put his cowardice aside and tell Annie that he loved her and wanted to remarry.

For the rest of the day Ian could barely concentrate on his report for the board. His mind constantly wandered to the upcoming meeting with Annie. He'd been a fool to give her up without a fight. Throughout the rest of the day, he worked on spread sheets and met with the chef at the senior center, who gave a positive account of the new food vendor. He did his best to push aside thoughts of Annie, but the discussions about the finances brought the approaching meeting with her front and center. When he returned to his office a little before five o'clock, he was exhausted from trying not to think about her.

Sitting at his desk, Ian pulled out a little black case from the top drawer. He opened the case and stared at the engagement ring. He'd bought it the day after the hostage crisis, figuring the purchase would keep him from chickening out with Annie. If she said yes, this ring would signify a fresh start for both of them.

Five-thirty came and went and Annie hadn't arrived, but the pizza had. He paced in front of his desk. Had something happened to her, or had she changed her mind? Maybe something had happened to one of the kids. He shook his head. Why did he have to imagine every horrible scenario? He reached for his phone and punched in her number. Ringing sounded in his ear. No answer. Voice mail.

"Ian."

He looked at his phone. He wasn't connected.

"What are you doing?" A chuckle sounded in Annie's voice.

Ian spun around. His heart lodged in his throat. Annie's blue eyes sparkled with life—the new life she had forged with God at her side. He wanted more than anything to be part of that life. Sharing his love with this woman who was beautiful inside and out would make his life complete. She was everything he needed. "You're here. I just tried to call you. Then I heard your voice, and it confused me."

Annie smiled like she knew something he didn't. "Do we eat first or talk?"

"Eat. I don't like cold pizza." He went to the desk and opened the pizza box next to the paper plates. Plus, he needed more time to prepare himself for what he planned to do.

They ate and talked some about their workday. Annie told him about the success of her parents' visit. She seemed happy. They were having a congenial conversation. Was he going to upset everything with his proposal? He needed to get her finance discussion out of the way before he talked himself out of this declaration of his love.

He put his half-eaten slice of pizza on the plate. "What do you have to tell me about the finances? I hope it's good news."

"It's better than good. It's fantastic, stupendous, marvelous and a godsend." Annie reached into her purse and brought out an envelope. "Here. Take a look."

Ian opened the envelope and pulled out a check. He blinked, then blinked again. His mouth dropped open. He looked at Annie. "From your parents?"

Smiling, she nodded. "I told you it was fabulous news."

He grinned so broadly that he didn't think his face could contain it. He took Annie's hand and pulled her to her feet, then twirled her around the room. When he stopped, he put his hands on her shoulders. "This means we can pay off debts and have money left over."

"And I have a plan to put the leftover money in a trust. I want to run it by you tonight and then the finance committee tomorrow before we present it to the board."

"Wonderful, but I have something to say before you tell me about your plan."

Annie stepped away and held up both hands in front of her. "I have something to say, too. Ladies first, right?"

"Okay, ladies first." If she kept finding ways to put him off, would he lose his nerve?

Annie took a deep breath, then licked her lips. "I've said some of this before, but I want to say it one more time. I'm sorry I ruined our marriage. I'm thankful that you've forgiven me, and I want to…I want to start over."

"I—"

"Please let me finish." Annie held up one hand.

"Okay." His heart raced. She wanted to start over. That was a good sign.

"I'm sorry, too, about the way I reacted the other day. You saved my life. I was on a path to ruin. If not for what you did, I might have died of an overdose. Losing Kara and Spencer was a turning point for me. I had to get help. Forgive me again?" Annie held her breath.

"I should've told you from the beginning." Ian shook his head. "But I never thought we'd come to a point where we wanted to be together again. Where do we go from here?"

Her heart thudding, Annie finally breathed. "I don't want to waste any more time being apart. I love you, Ian Montgomery. Kara told me you said you'd marry me and be a daddy to my kids if I asked you. So I'm asking. Will you marry me again?"

Ian stood there, stunned, his mouth hanging open again. She had beaten him to the proposal. Bless little Kara.

"I'm sorry if Kara put words in your mouth. I'm sorry if I put you on the spot with my proposal." Annie dropped her gaze to the floor.

Ian went down on one knee in front of Annie. He looked up into her face. "You didn't put me on the spot. You just beat me to it. I love you, and I love your kids. I want to start over, too. I'll marry you and be a daddy to your children." He fished in his pocket for the ring case. He pulled it out and popped it open. "I bought this for you."

Annie put her hands over her mouth and cried and laughed at the same time as Ian stood up and pulled her into his arms. When he let her go, she stepped back and held out her left hand. Ian placed the ring on her finger. Standing on her tiptoes, she flung her arms around his neck. "Thank you for loving me and my kids. I don't deserve you, but I'm glad God saw fit to bring us back together."

"Let's get Kara and Spencer so we can tell them they get to have a new daddy."

"Good idea, but one thing before we go." Ian took Annie in his arms and kissed her, then kissed her again. He held her close. "With God in our lives, we'll make it work this time."

When their embrace ended, Annie smiled up at him. "God has certainly taken a lot of bad stuff and turned it into something good."

"Amen to that." Ian took Annie's hand in his. "We're living proof."

* * * * *

Dear Reader

Thank you for choosing to read *Second Chance Reunion*. This is the first in a series of books set in my imaginary multifaceted ministry for those in need, The Village of Hope. In Matthew 25:39–40, Jesus gives us an example of caring for those in need. James 1:27 says, "Religion that God our Father accepts as pure and faultless is this: to look after orphans and widows in their distress and to keep oneself from being polluted by the world."

I hope you enjoyed Annie's journey to restore her family and Ian's journey to forgive. Both of them learned how God can take our mistakes and turn them into something good. This story of two flawed people reminds us that God makes everything new when we accept His grace. We can also know that God uses imperfect people to accomplish His tasks here on earth. Please look for future books in The Village of Hope series.

I enjoy hearing from readers. You can reach me through my website: www.merrilleewhren.com. Or you can write to me through the Harlequin Readers Service.

Merrillee Whren

Questions for Discussion

1. At the beginning of the story Annie wonders whether The Village of Hope will be a good place for her. Why do you think she has this question? Discuss a time when you went to a place or event that caused you some anxiety.

2. When Annie and Ian meet again, the situation is awkward. Discuss how you think each of them was feeling. Have you ever encountered someone with whom you've had a disagreement? Discuss how this made you feel.

3. Annie finds a friend in Cora. Why do you think Annie is drawn to the older woman? Discuss how different generations can be a help to each other.

4. Ian and his father don't agree on some subjects. Do you think Ian did the right thing when he avoided discussing these subjects? Why or why not? Do you think it is better to avoid discussing things that people don't agree on? Why or why not?

5. Why do you think both Annie and Ian had problems forgetting their past mistakes? Are

there mistakes you have made that you constantly remember? If so, how do you handle it? Is it important to put the past behind you? Why or why not?

6. Annie's parents weren't very involved in her life while she was growing up. Although her brother grew up under the same circumstances, he did not rebel. Why do you think children in the same family don't always behave in the same way?

7. Do you think Ian should have felt guilty for reporting Annie to DFCS? Why or why not?

8. Forgiveness is a big theme in this story. What part does forgiveness play in reconciliation?

LARGER-PRINT BOOKS!

GET 2 FREE
LARGER-PRINT NOVELS
PLUS 2 FREE
MYSTERY GIFTS

Love Inspired®
SUSPENSE
RIVETING INSPIRATIONAL ROMANCE

Larger-print novels are now available...

YES! Please send me 2 FREE LARGER-PRINT Love Inspired® Suspense novels and my 2 FREE mystery gifts (gifts are worth about $10). After receiving them, if I don't wish to receive any more books, I can return the shipping statement marked "cancel." If I don't cancel, I will receive 4 brand-new novels every month and be billed just $5.24 per book in the U.S. or $5.74 per book in Canada. That's a savings of at least 23% off the cover price. It's quite a bargain! Shipping and handling is just 50¢ per book in the U.S. and 75¢ per book in Canada.* I understand that accepting the 2 free books and gifts places me under no obligation to buy anything. I can always return a shipment and cancel at any time. Even if I never buy another book, the two free books and gifts are mine to keep forever.

110/310 IDN F5CC

Name	(PLEASE PRINT)

Address	Apt. #

City	State/Prov.	Zip/Postal Code

Signature (if under 18, a parent or guardian must sign)

Mail to the Harlequin® Reader Service:
IN U.S.A.: P.O. Box 1867, Buffalo, NY 14240-1867
IN CANADA: P.O. Box 609, Fort Erie, Ontario L2A 5X3

**Are you a current subscriber to Love Inspired Suspense books
and want to receive the larger-print edition?
Call 1-800-873-8635 or visit www.ReaderService.com.**

* Terms and prices subject to change without notice. Prices do not include applicable taxes. Sales tax applicable in N.Y. Canadian residents will be charged applicable taxes. Offer not valid in Quebec. This offer is limited to one order per household. Not valid for current subscribers to Love Inspired Suspense larger-print books. All orders subject to credit approval. Credit or debit balances in a customer's account(s) may be offset by any other outstanding balance owed by or to the customer. Please allow 4 to 6 weeks for delivery. Offer available while quantities last.

Your Privacy—The Harlequin® Reader Service is committed to protecting your privacy. Our Privacy Policy is available online at www.ReaderService.com or upon request from the Harlequin Reader Service.

We make a portion of our mailing list available to reputable third parties that offer products we believe may interest you. If you prefer that we not exchange your name with third parties, or if you wish to clarify or modify your communication preferences, please visit us at www.ReaderService.com/consumerschoice or write to us at Harlequin Reader Service Preference Service, P.O. Box 9062, Buffalo, NY 14269. Include your complete name and address.

ReaderService.com

Manage your account online!

- Review your order history
- Manage your payments
- Update your address

> ### We've designed the Harlequin® Reader Service website just for you.

Enjoy all the features!

- Reader excerpts from any series
- Respond to mailings and special monthly offers
- Discover new series available to you
- Browse the Bonus Bucks catalog
- Share your feedback

Visit us at:

ReaderService.com